The Regan McHenry Real Estate Mysteries
The Death Contingency
Backyard Bones
Buying Murder
The Widow's Walk League
The Murder House
A Neighborly Killing

PIP Inc. Mysteries
The Glass House
The Funeral Murder
The Corpse's Secret Life
Dearly Beloved Departed
Donor 73101

Other books by Nancy Lynn Jarvis
Mags and the AARP Gang

Edited Anthologies
**Cozy Food: 128 Cozy Mystery Writers Share Their
Favorite Recipes
Santa Cruz Weird
Santa Cruz Ghost Stories**

The Two-Faced Triplex

A Regan McHenry Real Estate Mystery

Nancy Lynn Jarvis
Good Read Mysteries
An imprint of Good Read Publishers

Good Read Publishers
301 Azalea Lane, Santa Cruz, California, 95060

Copyright © 2018 by Nancy Kille

Library of Congress Control Number: 2018930206

ISBN: 978-0-9973667-2-3

Good Read Publishers, Second Edition, Revised August 2020

Printed in the United States of America

www.nancylynnjarvis.com

Books are available at special quantity discounts through the website.

For my late husband, Craig. I'm having a good life like I promised I would. Writing is a big part of that, of course, but the writing was so much more fun when you read my words before anyone else did.

Acknowledgments

Thank you to Dan at DeLavega Golf Course and the other workers there who told me how golf carts work and were disappointed that I wasn't really going to kill someone on site.

Thank you to my friend Pat Pfremmer for her intriguing idea.

Thank you to Carmel Realtor Christine Handel for her stories about the real estate scene there.

A special thank you goes to Morgan Rankin for her editing and encouragement.

And a special thanks to Sam Burke the Chevalier King Charles Spaniel who lent me his likeness and name.

The Two-Faced Triplex

A Regan McHenry Real Estate Mystery

Nancy Lynn Jarvis

It never starts out like what I'm doing is going to get me into trouble, but it always does. You'd think I'd have learned that by now.

Regan McHenry

Amanda, the receptionist at Kiley and Associates — the real estate company Regan co-owned with her husband, Tom — had a touch of urgency and a great deal of pride in her voice as she spoke over the office intercom.

"Visitor headed your way, Regan. She wouldn't stop to give a name, but she seems to know where your office is so she must have been here before. That's my deduction, anyway."

Regan could hear the smile on Amanda's face, present because of her Sherlock-like observation, part of her new-found alertness after Regan and Tom asked her to help with a sting operation the month before.

Regan rose from her chair and hurried to her office door, ready to greet her visitor. She got to the entrance just in time to be engulfed by a sobbing woman who was petite enough that, when she threw her arms around Regan, her head rested on Regan's chest.

Remembering names, even the names of former clients like the distraught young woman was, had never been Regan's strong suit, but in this instance, she did remember, not only who she was, but also her name. The anguished woman was the daughter of one of Regan's favorite clients, Martha Varner, and she had an unusual and, therefore, memorable name.

"Mom's dead, the police say she killed herself, and I'm going to lose everything. Please, Regan, you've got to help me. Jackson and I are going to be out..." she trailed off in gulping sobs... "on the street."

Regan put her arms around the distressed woman and spoke sympathetically, "Mireya, I'm so sorry about your mom, so sorry, so sorry," while, like a dancer leading a partner in a slow foxtrot, she guided her charge until they reached the sofa in her office. "Sit down and tell me what's happened."

Regan pressed the anguished woman down onto the sofa, relinquishing her hold only long enough to move to her desk, buzz her receptionist — "Amanda, we need tea, please,"— and pick up the tissue box that resided there, before joining her grief-stricken visitor on the sofa.

"Take a deep breath and tell me what's going on," Regan said as she held out the tissue box.

After a few more snuffles, Mireya regained enough control to speak without crying. "I'm so sorry to bother you with this, but it's about...it's kind of a real estate issue, you know, and I thought of you. And you were so kind and helped us so much when Mom gave me the loan for my house...and I know you liked my mother...she liked you, too. She always said you were her trusted real estate agent..."

The flood of tears returned with a vengeance. "You're a busy woman and it's been six months since I bought my house. I was worried you wouldn't remember us."

"How could I forget Jackson? He's such a cutie. Last time I saw him he was just taking his first steps."

Mireya took a tissue and dabbed at her tears. "He runs now." A resolute smile appeared on Mireya's face as she mentioned her son. "Mom loved him so much; she'd never risk his home. And she'd never end her life without saying goodbye to us."

"Your mother showed me pictures of him every time we ran into one another. What happened?"

"I got the call from the Capitola police on Wednesday. They said Mom's next-door neighbor, Judi Pardini, her buddy, found her body. They think Mom probably died late in the day on Tuesday. The police said there was an empty pill bottle next to her." Tears filled Mireya's eyes. She dabbed at them, but it was a losing battle and they cascaded down her cheeks.

"The first call I made when I heard was to her doctor. I asked straight out if she had prescribed anything my mother could have ODed on. She wouldn't tell me much because of confidentiality rules, but she said my mom was healthy for her age, with no signs of cancer or dementia — those were the things Mom always feared — and nothing more going on than arthritis and the normal creaks and groans of a sixty-eight-year-old woman."

"It sounds like physically she was fine, but..."

Mireya covered Regan's words with a burst of her own. "Everyone says what you're about to. My mother was not depressed. I talked with her just last Monday, the day before she died. She was really excited. She said she had amazing news to tell me and a surprise, two surprises in fact, that she couldn't wait to share. She said the surprises were too big to

4

say over the phone. She told me to get a sitter for Jackson — which was so unlike her; she'd never miss a chance to see him — and meet her in Carmel at the Mission Ranch for lunch on Saturday. She laughed and said things were going so well, we'd probably see Clint Eastwood in the bar. Does that sound like something someone so depressed that she was planning to kill herself would say?"

Regan shook her head. "No, it certainly doesn't."

"And then yesterday, I got the call from a realtor in Carmel. She said Mom was involved in the purchase of property there, that she'd used her condo near the Village and the note for my house as payment for the purchase, and that she'd removed all the contingencies from the contract and signed all the escrow papers. The realtor said that meant there was no way to stop escrow from closing and that Mom's condo would become the property of the seller.

"The note on my house read that monthly payments were to be made for thirty years until the note was paid off or the house was sold. If the house was sold or if Mom died, the note was due and payable within thirty days. In her trust Mom stipulated my note was to be forgiven if she died, but the realtor said Mom changed her trust recently, deleting the part about it being forgiven. I checked with Mom's attorney and he said the realtor was right.

"So now, unless I pay off the note in full, which is something I can't do, the seller is entitled to take my house, too. Regan, what am I going to do?"

"Even if the realtor said there was no way to stop the sale, that may not be the case. Let me go over your mother's copy of the purchase contract and see if I can spot anything that might help you."

"You know how well-organized Mom was. I've looked in her desk and anywhere else that seems remotely like where she'd keep important papers, but I can't find it."

Amanda arrived with a tray holding two cups and a teapot. "I know you didn't say to, Regan, but I decided to make green tea from Japan. I thought it might be soothing."

Mireya stared up at Amanda. "You're so perceptive."

"Thank you, Amanda. Green tea is just what we need," Regan added.

Once the tea was poured, Regan offered, "I'm not sure if I can help, Mireya, but I'll certainly try. If you'll give me the name of the realtor who called you, I can make a call and see what I can find out."

"Thank you so much. I'm overwhelmed on so many levels and now I have a memorial service to plan. Judi's helping me, though, so I don't have to do it all on my own."

"You don't have any siblings to help?"

"No. I was a late in life surprise. Mom always said she didn't think she could have children, so she and my dad considered me their miracle baby. That's why they named me Mireya. It means miracle. The realtor's name is Roya Matthews. I was so shaken that I didn't write down her phone number or the name of the company she's with. Sorry."

"No problem. I'm sure I can find her."

Regan and Mireya sipped their tea and reminisced about her mom during happier times, but as soon as she left, Regan turned to her computer and entered "roya matthews carmel realtor." Her screen filled with links. Regan selected RoyaMatthews.com and was rewarded with a flashy, professional page.

A banner proclaimed Roya's membership in the top producer's club at Carmel Properties, the brokerage where she worked. A sliding column down the left side of the page listed her charitable committee memberships and showed her attending meetings, cutting ribbons, and grinning with local personalities, important community figures, and even superstars like Betty White and Robert Redford, who quietly owned property in Carmel. Testimonials, complete with photos of happy clients, scrolled across the bottom of the page. It was a lively, almost overwhelming array, but front and center was a glamorous still photo of Roya Matthews — her hair and the gossamer scarf wrapped around her neck apparently being blown back slightly to artistic advantage by an unseen wind machine — looking engagingly over her slightly angled shoulder and smiling warmly at the viewer. Regan thought the photo subliminally projected stability and reliability amid a sea of chaos. *Nicely done*, she chuckled to herself.

Regan noted the phone number displayed under Roya's motto, "I make your dreams come true," and punched it into her phone's keypad. After three rings, she was greeted by a husky voice saying that Roya Matthews was so sorry to have missed her call, but promising, if she left her name and number, a real live Roya would get back to her within two hours.

"Hi Roya," Regan started her message, "This is Regan McHenry from Kiley and Associates in Santa Cruz. Could you give me a call, please?" She concluded by leaving her cell number.

Regan's cell phone rang almost immediately.

"Regan, this is Roya," the voice Regan remembered from the outgoing message crooned warmly. "I just know we're going to work wonderfully well together. We'll probably be best friends by the time we finish the transaction. Which one of my listings in your buyer interested in?"

"I wish I had a buyer for one of your listings," Regan put a smile in her voice, "but I don't. I'm calling on behalf of my former clients, now friends, Martha Varner, and her daughter, Mireya."

"Oh, I see." The curtness of her response caused Regan to imagine the woman seen on Roya's webpage straightening up in her seat, elevating her chin, and entwining her fingers in her scarf.

"Mireya's quite upset about her mother, of course."

"Of course."

"She has a young child and she's concerned about the impact of her mother's death on their future because of the way her mother's trust was structured."

Roya sighed loudly. "I haven't met her, but from our phone conversation I suspect she's a bit of a drama queen. Don't you agree, if she's worried about her inheritance, she should take up her estate concerns with her mother's attorney and not either of us?"

"I'm sure she will. But for right now, I was hoping you could tell me about the contract Martha had so I can explain it to Mireya."

"Tell her to read, with your help if she must have it, her mother's copy of the contract."

"Mireya's searched through her mother's papers but she can't seem to find Martha's copy. It would be helpful if you could email one to my office."

"I'd like to help you and Martha's daughter, but I'm not sure about the ethics of that. I'm double-ending the sale. Since I'm representing the seller as well as Martha Varner, let me speak to the seller and see how he feels about what you're asking. I'll get back to you."

🏠🏠🏠🏠🏠🏠🏠🏠🏠🏠🏠🏠

Regan sat at the weekly office meeting her husband, as broker and co-owner of the company, was conducting for the agents in the office to present their new listings and give updates about selling prices and sales, absentmindedly drumming three fingers of her left hand on the cloth of her chair handle. *Tap, tap, ring finger, tap, middle finger, tap, index finger, repeat.*

Tom noticed her distraction. "Your friend Martha's funeral is this afternoon, isn't it?" he asked as the meeting broke up and agents headed to their cars for the new listing tour.

"It is. I was hoping to have some news for her daughter, ideally good news to make the day easier for her, but I'm not getting any cooperation from Martha's Carmel agent. I've called her and texted her, but she's ignoring me."

"Being a pushy agent are you, without any authority to do so?" Tom teased. "Maybe she thinks you're after a cut of her commission."

"Please," Regan scowled.

"Your uncooperative agent is with Carmel Properties, isn't she? Do you want me to call her broker and see if he'll nudge her a bit?"

"Have you met him at a regional broker conference or, better yet, played a round of golf with him?"

"No. I've never met him."

"Then I don't think you should. But," Regan made the word longer by half than it was, "tomorrow is our day off. You could take me to lunch in Carmel tomorrow and we could just sort of turn up at Roya Mathew's office," she giggled.

"It sounds like we have a date."

Regan arrived early at the Oakwood Chapel where Martha's memorial service was being held. The chapel was still mostly empty, but the venue was on the small side and she expected that Martha had many friends who would want to remember her. Since she didn't want to risk taking an important place, Regan picked an aisle seat in the last row.

From her vantage point, Regan noted there were a few scattered blondes and brunettes present, but gray-haired mourners were in the majority. Judging by the age of most of the attendees, Regan thought she must be one of Martha's newer friends. She was surprised, though, that so many of the seats remained empty.

The service was nondenominational and a representative from the chapel, who clearly had never met Martha, read a brief synopsis of her life in a decorous monotone. He droned on about her parents — like her daughter, Martha had been an only child — where she grew up, her education, her marriage to Mireya's father and her widowhood four years before, the joy Mireya's birth brought and how wonderful grandson Jackson's arrival had been for her, and listed all of the charities Martha supported. It was a dry recital, especially for someone as delightful, warm, and interesting as Martha had been. Regan was relieved when his words trailed off.

"Oh my God," a silver-haired woman from the front row who was dressed, not in dark mourning colors, but in bright red and purple, jumped to her feet and seized the microphone from his hand. "Martha lived, relished life, and enjoyed it fully," she exclaimed, "but you'd never know it from listening to him, would you?

"I'm Judi Pardini, Martha's best friend." She surveyed the room with a raised eyebrow and a mischievous smile on her face. "Now, I know many of you think you should have that title. After all, to Martha there were no strangers, only people she wasn't best friends with yet, but I'm the one she shared *all* her secrets with and I bet none of you can say that. If you want to challenge me, please do; let's hear from you. Who's first up to tell a Martha story?"

Heads turned and people squirmed, but no one rose. Regan hadn't intended to, but she didn't mind public speaking and thought perhaps she should say something to break the ice. She was about to accept Judi Pardini's prompt when Martha's friend began speaking once more.

"Oh, I know. This is a difficult situation," Judi continued, this time without mirth. "Martha treasured the friendship of all of you who are here. Being Martha, she would have still prized the friendship of those who didn't come, but her heart would have broken a bit that they couldn't bring themselves here to pay their respect. Knowing what to say and what to do when a loved-one passes is always difficult, but suicide adds to that burden and we all know the police believe Martha committed suicide.

"Every one of you in this chapel knows what zest for life Martha had, so I want to reassure all of you who did come here today. I don't believe Martha committed suicide. Not for a minute. Martha wouldn't do that, especially not now. Martha didn't commit suicide; she was murdered."

An animated Regan narrated the story of Martha Varner's memorial service to Tom as he drove them down Highway 1 toward Carmel. "So you can imagine what happened after Judi said that Martha was murdered."

"I can, but I bet what really happened was more interesting than anything I can imagine."

"Oh, it was something, alright." Regan raced on with her account. "Mireya jumped up — she was sitting several seats away from where Judi had been seated, which seemed odd to me because Mireya said Judi was helping her plan the memorial service so I would have expected them to be supporting one another and sitting next to one another — and yanked the microphone out of Judi's hand. Judi didn't give it up lightly so there was some physical wrangling involved.

"Once she had the mic firmly in control, Mireya offered a breathy, 'Oh my, Mom's suicide has been so hard on all of us, we're all overwrought and imaging all sorts of things.' Then she did her best to calm everything down by appealing to another friend of Martha's and asked her to share a remembrance of volunteering at the SPCA together."

"Did it work?"

"More or less. Judi sat down again and other stories followed, so the service returned to a normal state, but Judi left as soon as the chapel representative announced a light lunch was being served next door and suggested people move to that space. Granted, I didn't stay long, but I heard a lot more talk about Judi's outburst than I did about Martha's life before I left."

Tom turned off Highway 1. "Unless you're starving, I'm going to take the Ocean Street exit instead of going to Rio Road. Carmel Properties is on Dolores. Let's go by and see if Roya Matthews is there. If she isn't, we can have lunch and kill time until she's expected."

Regan nodded.

"When we see her, do you want me to be quiet or intimidating? Your call," Tom grinned.

"Quiet, I think. But if I scratch my nose like this," Regan demonstrated with a laugh, "take her out."

While the suit-wearing receptionist announced, "Mr. and Mrs. Kiley to see you, Roya," Regan glanced around the imposing office. It was designed to be Carmel quaint on the outside, but it was sleek and modern on the inside. The artwork on the walls was expensive. She wondered if gallery owners let the real estate company use pieces for free or if they made the company buy it. Carmel Properties catered to high-end buyers and sellers; she'd take a bet on the first option.

A tall woman Regan recognized immediately from her webpage came toward them from one of the nearby offices. Regan tried to guess her age and decided she might be anywhere from mid-forties to early fifties, but it was hard to tell her age exactly because her makeup was perfect and extremely flattering. She was trim and was dressed from head to toe in gold-colored clothing — stiletto pumps, suit with three-quarter sleeves, and scarf at her neck — but the fabrics and finishes were subdued and, except for the scarf which had glistening golden threads woven into it and her heavy gold woven-rope bracelet which sparkled, the effect was to make Roya look not brassy but like a golden goddess. An expensive one.

"Mr. and Mrs. Kiley," she cupped their extended hands in turn with both of hers, "I'm delighted to meet you. Please come into my office and have some coffee, or something stronger if you'd like,' she winked and chortled as she talked, "and tell me what I can do for you today."

"We've spoken on the phone, Roya." Regan matched the size of Roya Mathew's smile with her own as she and Tom took seats in the office. "I usually introduce myself as Regan McHenry rather than Mrs. Kiley, though. Tom and I were in the neighborhood today and thought we'd stop by because I seem to keep missing your returned phone calls. You know, the ones about getting a copy of Martha Varner's purchase contract? I believe you were going to ask the seller if that was alright with him."

"Yes, well I did leave him a message, but he's such a busy man that we can go months between touching base. That's why I haven't returned your call. No news. All the necessary documents have been signed — Martha made a trip to Carmel last week to sign hers — and escrow is scheduled to close soon, so it's too late to change anything anyway."

"What about Mireya?"

"Humph," Roya snorted. "Little miss drama queen. Don't worry about her. Martha insisted the contract stipulate she had six months of occupancy under the same terms she had with her mother. Martha thought they could both...I've said too much already. Tell the daughter, she'll have plenty of time to find a new place to live."

"Regan, do you have Mireya's phone number with you?" Tom asked.

"I do," Regan responded as she reached into her purse and retrieved her cell phone.

"Give her a call. Ask her for the phone number of the attorney handling her mother's estate." He smiled warmly at Roya. "Roya will need it to get information about Martha's property purchase to the attorney, who will also need a copy of the purchase contract and contact information of the seller so Mireya will know where her monthly mortgage payments are to be sent. You could wait until escrow closes, I suppose, before releasing anything to the attorney, but then time will be of the essence, so I would think you'll be better advised to take care of those details as soon as you have a chance, even if you haven't heard from your client."

"You don't need to call the daughter. I have all that information ready to go. I'll be sure to get it to her in a timely manner."

"Glad to hear that we can count on you, Roya," Tom said.

As they sat at the Mission Ranch Restaurant, Regan used her fork to emphasize her point before she plunged it into her Cobb salad once more. "I don't trust her to do anything she promised. I've got a bad feeling about her; she's hiding something."

"You're overreacting. She likes to be in charge and she doesn't see why you should be butting into her territory, even if Mireya asked you to, that's all."

Regan shook her head. "You're just blinded by her perfectly turned-out outfit and how attractive she is." She half-way meant what she said, although her mouth turned up at the edges.

"I didn't notice what she was wearing, but I did notice she's a very attractive woman," he retorted in the same spirit.

"Roya Matthews knows a lot more than she's saying and I…"

"Don't want to get involved," Tom tried to finish her sentence for her.

"Not exactly what I was going to say," Regan chuckled, "but for now you're probably putting the right words in my mouth."

"Why do I have the intense feeling you're going to replace trying to get something out of Roya with doing something else you shouldn't?"

"I'm not going to do anything you'll disapprove of; I'm just going to have a little chat with Judi Pardini. Aren't you as curious as I am to know why she said what she did at Martha's memorial service?"

"I could say no, but I know better than think my opinion matters; I'm sure you're curious enough for both of us."

🏠🏠🏠🏠🏠🏠🏠🏠🏠🏠🏠🏠

Regan got Judi's phone number from Mireya when she called to give her an update about what she and Tom learned in Carmel. While the news she delivered wasn't particularly good, at least she was able to reassure Mireya that her world wasn't going to crash around her feet immediately.

Judi answered her phone after three rings.

"Hello, Mrs. Pardini, my name is Regan McHenry. I'm a real estate agent and Martha Varner was a client of mine who became a friend. I was at Martha's memorial service and heard what you said. I was wondering if we could talk."

"Real estate agent, you said? Are you the one from Santa Cruz or the one from Carmel?"

"The one from Santa Cruz."

"In that case, I'll talk to you. How does tomorrow at 8 o'clock sound? Sorry I can't make it any later in the day, but we may need an hour and I'm booked solid later in the day and I know how you real estate agents don't like to be put off."

Regan smiled to herself, *Judi Pardini sounds like she could keep up with Martha.* "8:00 is fine. I have an early morning tomorrow, too."

"If you come to my place, I'll make you French toast for breakfast. I make a mean platter of French toast. My condo is next door to Martha's, on the left if you take the elevator, on the right if you take the stairs."

"I'll come hungry," Regan promised.

"Come on in." Judi, again dressed in red and purple, this time in a kaftan-like get-up, moved out of her doorway and motioned Regan inside.

"Head to the kitchen," Judi pointed the way. "I know how real estate agents like to sit at the kitchen table to talk — I was one briefly, oh, let me think, it's been forty years ago — and I still remember that from a seminar I went to." Judi adopted an exaggerated manner of speaking. "'Get people sitting around the kitchen table and they'll think of you on friendly terms and talk more freely, and be willing to sign on the bottom line.'" Judi erupted with laughter. "Besides, that's where the French toast is."

Regan swiveled her head as she walked toward the kitchen. Judi's living room was crammed with plants and photos of dogs and cats, each photo propped on top of or next to a small urn.

Judi spoke quickly and briskly as they walked. "I can't help but noticing you noticing my habitat. I used to have dogs. When I had to put Rocky, my sweet little Pomeranian, down, I couldn't bear to get another dog, so I got a cat. I never really liked cats — at least that's what I thought until I had one, then two, then seven — and when the last one died, I switched to green things. It turns out, you can get pretty attached to plants, too, but you don't have to walk them or clean their litter box, so they're a good match for an old lady like me. But you can't pet plants or pet ashes, so now I volunteer at the SPCA like Martha did, to get my daily fur fix. Have a seat."

Judi took a cast iron pan out of her oven and dished out two pieces of French toast for each of them. She slathered on butter and presented Regan with her plate. Coffee was already made and on the table, being kept warm by the plugged in coffee maker.

"Help yourself to syrup if you must, but I think a squeeze of lemon and a sprinkling of powdered sugar tastes better."

Regan chose lemon and sugar and was rewarded by a delicious burst of flavor when she took her first bite. "Umm. Cinnamon?" she asked.

"Yes, and just a grind of cardamom. Like I told you, I'm a busy woman so let's get right to the point. Why did you want to talk to me?"

Regan decided to be as direct as Judi was. "I was at Martha's memorial service and heard what you said. Murder is a pretty big charge. All indications are Martha took her own life; why do you think she was murdered?"

"Two reasons. First, she was absolutely ecstatic about her recent discovery. She swore me to secrecy until she could get everyone together. But that's not going to happen now — Martha didn't share enough information about the players that I can make it happen — and anyway, I don't think sworn secrets go beyond the grave. Not when there's murder involved."

"I'm inclined to agree," Regan said. "What was her big discovery?"

"You need a little history first, and you're sitting down so this is the perfect time for you to hear it. Mireya is not Martha's only child. She had a boy before she and Mireya's father met."

"A boy? But Martha never mentioned him," Regan stuttered.

"No, she didn't. Not to anyone but me. And even with me, it took till after Jackson's birth before she told me everything, and we'd been best friends for more than thirty years.

"Martha sort of broke down one day after Mireya got pregnant without a wed-locked daddy in the picture and kinda accidentally said 'like mother, like daughter.' She said she didn't mean to say anything and made a slip before she thought about what she was saying. I don't believe that for a second. I think Martha wanted to tell someone for a long time, but felt she had to bear her burden by herself as a kind of atonement or punishment — or whatever the right word is — for what she did."

"What happened to her child?"

"She put him up for adoption the day he was born. She said she didn't even want to see him for fear she'd change her mind. Then along came Jackson. Martha was terrified Mireya would do the same thing she did and live to regret it. But times are different now and Mireya kept her baby.

"Martha was so pleased, but every time she saw that little tyke, she wondered if that was what her boy looked like when he was little. Does it make sense to you that having Jackson in her life was the most wonderful and awful thing at the same time that could happen to her?"

"It does. Judi, maybe it got to be too much for her. Maybe that's why she ended her life," Regan suggested.

"You didn't let me finish my story. You know how adopted children sometimes search for their birth parents? Well, it seems her child contacted her a few months ago. Martha's on the board for the SPCA and she went to Monterey last May for their annual Wag n' Walk to scope it out because we were thinking of setting up a local version.

"Martha said a dog that looked just like hers, blenheim colored and all, started prancing along next to Queeny. Have you met Queeny, Martha's Chevalier King Charles Spaniel?"

"I have." Regan replied. "Queeny's as cute as dogs get."

"You wouldn't say that if you knew my Rocky. Anyway, this other Chevalier King Charles's owner started asking questions about the litter Queeny was from, suggesting maybe their dogs were litter mates — Martha said there's an active Chevalier King Charles breeder locally — which is what made her companion wonder. And it turns out, the other dog was named Queeny, too.

"They decided that was such a coincidence that, after the event, they headed to the Cypress Inn in Carmel — it seemed like the perfect dog friendly environment, especially since the other Queeny and her owner were from Carmel — for lunch and dog biscuits. Well, before long, guess what? The new Queeny's human started calling Martha mommy."

Judi pursed her lips and nodded. "Martha said she'd had a special feeling, felt a special closeness, all afternoon while they walked and talked. She even thought she saw a family resemblance between them. And then, when both dogs turned out to have the same name, she figured that was because both owners thought in the same way.

"So, Martha believed the whole long-lost-baby thing right away. She thought they had to be related; they had to be parent and child.

"Martha was so excited. And so delighted. She said she was going to have her whole little family together once and for all."

"Did she tell Mireya about her brother?"

"I don't think so. It's possible Martha let something slip, like she did with me, but on the whole, she was pretty darn good at keeping secrets. Martha said she was going to introduce Mireya and her lost baby in Carmel over lunch and she could hardly wait. So, you do see why she would never have ended her life now?"

All Regan could manage was, "Wow," as she leaned back in her seat and shook her heard. "Mireya said her mother wanted them to have lunch in Carmel and told her there was going to be a huge surprise revealed at that lunch. It all makes sense.

"Have you told Mireya about any of this, yet?"

"Not yet. It's a lot to drop on that girl so soon after she lost her mother. I'm kind of practicing on you to see how it sounds being said out loud before I do," Judi chuckled.

She turned pensive immediately. "Now, without Martha, the whole little family thing is off. All our plans have changed, even mine. It sure is good I didn't rush to list my condo. Martha told me to give you a call and I was going to, but I didn't get around to it."

"Why did Martha want you to sell your condo?"

"She said, since I was like a sister to her and an aunt to Mireya, she was sure I'd love her lost child — that's what she called him — and she wanted me to be part of her family. She waved a copy of her purchase contract for what she was buying in front of me and said there'd be room for me in Carmel with her and her children. She told me to read over the contract and I'd see what she meant."

It was doubtful Judi, who hadn't been a real estate agent for decades, would have discovered the out Regan hoped to find for Mireya, but she asked anyway. "Did you read it?"

"We were so busy talking that I didn't get around to it. Martha left it with me, though, so I could read it when I had a chance. Then she died and I never bothered to."

"Do you still have it?"

"It's here somewhere. I forget where I put it, though. Do you want me to look for it?"

"Yes, please. Mireya is worried that she may lose her house if the sale goes through. I told her I'd see if there's a way to stop the purchase, especially now that Martha's dead.

"What you've told me certainly qualifies as a reason to believe Martha didn't take her life, but you said you had two reasons to think she didn't. What's the other one?"

"She, well both of us, received a death threat. So, I know who killed Martha and I'm watching my back carefully, too."

Judi spoke matter-of-factly. Regan did not. "What?" Someone threatened her life? Who was it?"

"That no-good, animal abusing veterinarian who manages to get all of the SPCA's business." Judi's words were said softly but filled with venom. "He's been filing fraudulent invoices for care he never gave, spays he never performed, medicines he never injected. We have him dead to rights and sent off for the paperwork to file a formal complaint with the Veterinary Medical Board. His license is up for renewal and we planned to take him before the Board Disciplinary Committee.

"He found out what we were up to. I think some volunteer who thinks he's Doctor Wonderful overheard us scheming and tipped him off. Two weeks ago, when we were getting off our volunteer shifts, he grabbed us both by our arms," Judi held her elbow out at an angle to demonstrate how she was held, "scooted us outside to where our cars were parked and told us we better back off.

"Martha, well you know how feisty she was, said, 'Oh yeah? she said. 'And if we don't, what are you going to do about it?' and he said, if we didn't stop hassling him, we wouldn't be around for long."

"I'm not sure that what he said constitutes a death threat," Regan said hesitantly.

"You didn't hear the tone of his voice. It most certainly did."

"You didn't say what his name is. Are you willing to tell me?"

"You bet I am. William, 'Everybody calls me Dr. Billy,' Goatt."

Regan tried not to laugh as Judi pronounced the veterinarian's name, but she couldn't hide her amusement completely. "William Goat?"

"His last name has two tts at the end. Even so, he must have had some cruel parents to saddle him with William for a first name. Hard childhood. Maybe that's why he's such a no-good fraud."

🏠🏠🏠🏠🏠🏠🏠🏠🏠🏠🏠🏠

Sandy and her husband, Dave, who had invited Tom and Regan to their house for an impromptu dinner — an activity the couples who were best friends shared regularly — laughed out loud as they sipped a pre-dinner glass of wine and Regan told them about her meeting with Judi.

"Billy Goat?" Sandy repeated the name.

"No, no," Regan held up a finger and emphasized the second t as she spelled the name. "Goatt. G-o-a-t-T. I thought Judi really had some credible information about Martha being murdered, but clearly she's just missing her friend and filled with flamboyant ideas. I do see why she and Martha were buddies, though: Judi tells her stories in the most entertaining way and is a fireball like Martha was."

Dave, who earned his living as the Santa Cruz Police Department Ombudsman, scoffed. "I'm glad you think that, Regan, because when you started telling us your wild tale about another murder, I thought you were gonna' finish by telling us living in Santa Cruz had been a dream and we were really all from Midsomer County in England, like on that TV show. How many murders is it in that place? How many murders would this have been for you?" he teased sarcastically. "Maybe I should start practicing my British accent, just in case."

Sandy jumped up as the oven buzzer began to sound. "Perfect timing. The lasagna is ready, the salad's made, and the garlic bread just needs a sec under the broiler. Honey," she said to her husband, Dave, "you set the table." Sandy assigned tasks as only a good friend could do. "Tom, you open the wine you and Regan brought. Regan, you stand in

26

front of the oven and watch the bread; you know broiling the bread is my weak link and I tend to over-brown it."

"Do you mind if we turn on the TV while we get ready?" Regan asked. "It's time for local news and that roofer I like so much and have been recommending to clients turned up at a job wearing an ankle bracelet. Naturally, my clients called to let me know."

"Naturally," Tom interjected.

"I caught the last part of a news report on the radio when we were driving here, something about an ICE raid and undocumented immigrants being made to wear monitors. My roofer told me he was born in San Diego, but he may have made that up and may not be here legally. I want to hear the local news and see what I missed on the radio."

"I'd like to see that story, too," Dave said, as he used the remote to turn on the TV at the other end of the great room. "Everyone's talking about it. Chief said Santa Cruz police were lied to by Homeland Security and HS said sanctuary city or not, we knew what we were getting into with that raid a couple of weeks ago. Yeah, we all worked together and rounded up a dangerous gang, but about a dozen undocumented guys in the wrong place at the wrong time got detained and are now wearing monitors. No one knows what's gonna' happen to them.

"I tried to talk the Chief into letting me brief the media — that is part of my job — but he wanted to do it. So me and my best TV-Interviewee-Hawaiian-shirt had to stand down. I want to see how he did."

The flap caused by the raid was the top news story. Dave was about to click off the TV when it finished, but before he did, Regan heard a name she recognized in the lead-in to the next news item.

"Wait Dave," Regan said urgently and held up her hand.

"Mireya Varner has been detained on suspicion of murder in the death of her mother, Martha Varner," the reporter stated while a video of Mireya, head down on her way to a police car, played onscreen. "At this time, no motive has been released for the murder."

"What?" Regan shouted at the screen.

"Didn't the police say Martha took her own life?" Tom quizzed his friend.

"That's what Mireya told me," Regan added. She and Tom waited for an explanation from Dave.

"That was the theory, but an autopsy was ordered because the old lady died outside a doctor's care. Something must have turned up to change minds."

Dave puffed up his cheeks and blew out his breath in a slow huff. "Midsomer County, here we come after all. Good grief, Regan, how do you always manage to be in the middle of murder?"

"I'm not in the middle of anything, Dave," Regan protested.

"Right. You just happened to be telling us how the friend of your friend was telling you her friend was murdered and now she was, even though we thought she wasn't. And now it looks like your other friend and client, the one who came sobbing on your doorstep, did it.

"Tom, you wanna take my bet? Hundred-to-one-odds your wife can't keep her nose out of this one." He shook his head solemnly.

Tom looked from his wife to Dave and back again, wondering if Dave deliberately chose words knowing they would incite Regan or if he really was that ingenuous. "Not touching this," he laughed.

It was good Tom didn't take Dave's bet because he would have lost his dollar the moment Regan picked up her phone at work the next morning.

"Are you the same Regan who had breakfast with me yesterday?" Judi asked.

Regan would have recognized Judi's voice and tempo immediately even without the breakfast reference. "The same," she said.

"I figured you were. I didn't have your phone number, but I looked you up on the internet. There aren't that many Regans in Santa Cruz, especially Regans who are real estate agents.

"Have you heard about Mireya?" Judi didn't wait for Regan's answer. "She was arrested for Martha's murder. I told you Martha's death was murder, but what are those police thinking, arresting Mireya instead of Dr. Goatt?

"I tried calling them and telling them that, but I got shuttled off to some desk jockey and 'handled' like a crazy old bat."

Regan thought about Dave's full job description. As Santa Cruz Police Department Ombudsman, in addition to interfacing with the media, he was frequently the officer assigned to "cat in a tree" duty and talking to irate citizens. She had teased him often enough about the less than traditional policing duties he had to take on to remain on the force after losing his eye in a shootout.

"Do you remember the name of the officer you talked to?"

"You bet I do. Same name as my cousin: Everett."

"Judi, as it happens, I know him. Let me give him a call."

"Good morning, Dave," Regan said in a warm and friendly tone.

"Thirty-two minutes. Even faster than I expected." Dave's tone was neither warm nor friendly. It could only be described as disgruntled.

"I don't understand."

"I've been keeping track of the time, wondering how long it would be from, 'Goodbye, Mrs. Pardini' to 'Hello, Regan.' Thirty-two minutes. She ask you to call or did you volunteer?"

"When your name came up and I said I knew you...I volunteered."

"Ha! I knew you'd start meddlin'."

"I'm not meddling, Dave. I'm just surprised that Martha's death went from being a suicide to homicide. And Judi and I are both interested in why Mireya Varner is a suspect, since we both thought Martha and Mireya had such a close loving relationship. You can't call being curious meddling."

"Sure I can," he said firmly. "Okay, I've got a deal for you. It's all gonna' come out sooner or later anyway, but I know you're gonna' pester me until it does. So, if I tell you a couple of details before they get told to the news media, and you agree not to blab them to anyone until they become public, will you stop annoying me?"

"Absolutely."

He muttered, "Against my better judgment," under his breath, but loudly enough that Regan was sure to hear him. "There wasn't a suicide note, but there was an empty bottle of pills — Vicodin — next to the old lady's body."

"Mireya already told me that much."

"Seems your pal Martha had arthritis and her doc prescribed her Vicodin for occasional use. But the doc said she monitored refills and your pal Martha wasn't abusing the med. Our theory, though, was that she saved up her pills for a special occasion, like checking out. Some people, especially older people who have regular pain, have been known to do that. So, we made a suicide call.

"But there had to be an autopsy because the doc didn't sign off on your pal's death. The coroner did a basic toxicology screening as part of his autopsy. Turns out the tox screen didn't find any Vicodin in her. What turned up was diazepam, and here's the kicker, lots of insulin.

"Since her doc said the old lady wasn't a diabetic, the coroner took another look at her, and what do you know, they found an injection site in one of her armpits.

"Coroner figured somebody the old lady knew well enough to have a drink with got her so sedated on diazepam, she couldn't make a fuss and then shot her up with insulin. That's what killed her."

"But why do the police think it was Mireya?"

"Your gal Mireya had been pushing hard to have her mother's body cremated. Yeah, pushin' real hard, blubbering about her mom in a coroner's freezer and all and how it was weird keeping her mom on ice after her memorial service was held and all."

"That doesn't sound unreasonable, and it certainly doesn't sound like a good reason to suspect Mireya of her murder," Regan protested.

"I saved the best for last. Mireya Varner is a diabetic. Has been since she was a little girl. She uses insulin every day. Bada boom, bada bing."

🏠🏠🏠🏠🏠🏠🏠🏠🏠🏠🏠

Regan called Judi as soon as she got to her office and was relieved to get an answering machine. She was going to have to walk a serious tightrope reassuring Judi that the police had compelling, or at least reasonable, reasons to link Mireya to her mother's murder without breaking her word to Dave.

"Judi, I spoke with Dave Everett. It's early in the investigation, but it could be that…"

"I'm here. I was screening my calls. I feel safer that way."

Regan was caught. She went on, "As I was saying, it's early, but the police believe Martha was murdered and there is a connection between the method used and Mireya."

"I told you she was murdered," Judi said with a mixture of triumph and sadness. "How was she killed?"

Regan sighed to herself. *What should she say?* "Did you know Mireya is a diabetic?"

"Everyone knows that. She's type I."

"And you know she uses insulin?"

"She has to."

Judi was quiet for a few seconds, her quick mind processing Regan's questions and filling in the blanks. Judi gasped suddenly. "Martha was killed with insulin? If that's true, that's proof Dr. Goatt did it. I've got proof; I'll show you! Oh, he's going down and I'm going to relish letting him know he's going to pay for Martha."

"Judi, that doesn't sound like a good idea. Let the police have your evidence. I'm sure they'll take it seriously now and they can deal with him."

"And miss my chance to make him twist at the end of my rope? I'm just going to make a couple of phone calls — the last one will be to that nasty old Goatt — and then I'll be on my way to your office with my evidence. Oh, and I found Martha's purchase contract. I finally read it. I don't see any outs. Of course, it's been a long time since I read over a contract with a real estate agent's eye and the contracts were so different then. But even if the purchase goes through, the contract's not without interest; some of the names and connections in it are enticing. You still want to see it?"

"I do.

"Good. I'm putting it in the packet that's going to convict Dr. Goatt right now. I'm sure I'll be keyed up after I talk to that scoundrel and I don't want to forget it, because I have an interesting theory based on what Martha told me about her missing baby and… no point getting started on that right now; we can talk about it in person.

"Regan, I need to think about exactly what I'm going to say to that old Billy Goatt before I pick up the phone, so I'll be a little while. See you in a couple of hours?"

"I'll be waiting for you. Judi, would it be all right if I called Officer Everett to let him know we'll be in to see him later today?"

"If you promise me he won't treat me like I'm crazy."

"If you have evidence, I'm sure he won't."

"Then go ahead and call him, 'cause I do. Oh boy, this is going to be fun. I only wish Martha was here to be in on it."

🏠🏠🏠🏠🏠🏠🏠🏠🏠🏠🏠

When two hours had come and gone without Judi turning up, Regan dialed her phone number. She got the answering machine again, but this time as she left a message, Judi didn't pick up. *She's on her way.*

But when three hours passed without an appearance by Judi, Regan started to worry.

"Tom," Regan poked her head into her husband's office, "I need to run a quick errand. I'm expecting Judi Pardini at any moment and I've asked Amanda to call me if she turns up, but if she gets here before I get back, will you be charming and entertain her for a few minutes?"

"I'll do my best, Sweetheart, although I've got clients coming in at five."

35

"Oh, no problem. I'll be back way before then."

Regan checked the time as she started her car. It was only 1:27. The freeway wouldn't get crowded for at least half an hour. Even Mission Street should be quick to negotiate at this time of day. She could be in Capitola in twenty minutes, give or take, that is if she managed to get that far before Amanda called to say she should turn around because Judi was sitting in Tom's office explaining her Dr. Goatt vs. the SPCA fraud theories.

Regan promised herself she wouldn't feel foolish about overreacting to Judi's tardiness if Amanda did call her. What was the cliché? "Better safe than sorry?"

Regan made good time, parking at 850 Park Avenue a good fifteen minutes before 2 o'clock. Amanda hadn't intercepted her. She took the elevator that deposited her at the corner of the second floor where Martha's and Judi's condos, separated by stairs that ran the height of the building, afforded their owners impressive ocean views. She passed Martha's condo, which looked sad and lonely to her with its drawn drapes, and the staircase and prepared to knock on Judi's door. That's when she noticed the door was ever so slightly ajar.

Her heart began pounding as she took the door handle and pushed.

"Judi? Judi are you here?" Regan held her breath as she scanned the living room. She let herself in fully and moved to the kitchen. There was no sign of Judi. Regan shook her head and a small smile started across her mouth. *You sure can make up something wild out of nothing more than a woman not pulling her door completely closed, can't you?*

As she turned back toward the living room, Regan was able to see into Judi's bedroom. Lying in the very center of her neatly made bed was a still, small figure dressed colorfully in red and purple.

"Judi?" Regan whispered her name gently as if she hoped, by calling to her softly she could awaken the woman from her nap without startling her. But she knew better; Judi's lips were blue and she was waxy pale. She wasn't asleep.

Tears came with surprising rapidity. Regan's hand trembled as she reached into her purse, retrieved her cell phone, and called Dave's number.

"Officer Everett," he answered with a clipped business-only attitude. Hearing his professional tenor was comforting.

"Dave?" Regan spoke slowly, enunciating each word. "Dave, Judi Pardini is dead. I'm at her condo and she's dead."

Dave, who under some circumstances might have offered a snappy comeback about Regan calling to report yet another dead body, heard the stress and seriousness in her voice and didn't.

"Where are you?"

Regan gave him the address.

"That's Capitola police. I'll contact them. I don't need to tell you not to touch anything, do I?"

"No. I didn't touch anything, well nothing but the front doorknob when I didn't know Judi was dead."

"Do you want company?"

"Please!"

The urgency in her one-word reply told Dave just how unnerved she was. "I want you to go outside Judi's condo and wait there. A Capitola officer will be there soon. I'm on my way, but traffic will slow me down. Regan, sit down outside the condo, on the ground if you have to, especially if you feel queasy. We don't want you fainting. And Regan, call Tom while you wait."

"Unhuh."

Two uniformed Capitola police officers began bounding up the condo stairs within minutes. Regan could hear their hurrying feet on the steps before she saw them and was turned in their direction when they reached the second floor where she was. She had taken Dave's advice and was sitting down on the walkway in front of Judi's condo with her back against the building and her knees drawn up against her chest and held in place by her encircling arms.

"Are you hurt, ma'am?" the first officer asked as he put a hand on her shoulder.

"No. I'm fine. I don't do well finding dead bodies, is all," Regan offered a wan smile. "She's in the bedroom." As the officers started into the condo, Regan called after them, "I didn't touch anything."

Dave was next on the scene. He wasn't assigned a regulation police cruiser, and given how congested Highway 1 became after 2 o'clock, Regan wondered if he had used the portable bubble gum and siren he carried in his car to clear a path through traffic.

He gave her a wordless questioning look and held his thumb up in an okay sign. When she nodded, he disappeared inside the condo, too.

When Tom emerged from the elevator, Regan's attempt at composure ended. She was on her feet when he reached her and she crumpled into his arms.

"I'm here now, Sweetheart. It's all right."

Dave emerged from Judi's condo as Tom held his wife tightly.

"This place is being treated like a crime scene; it'll get a thorough look-see. The coroner is on his way. I told the Capitola officers I had taken your statement and would get a copy of it to them, so we can get out of here. Let's go somewhere where I really can take your statement, so I don't make a liar out of myself."

"Let's stop by Gayle's Bakery and get some coffee and chocolate into Regan," Tom suggested. "It should be reasonably quiet there at this time of day."

They sat at a table in the annex as far away from where the occasional patron placed an order for goodies as they could get and talked in hushed tones.

"Same setup as Martha Varner," Dave said. "No sign of forced entry, empty pill bottle on the nightstand next to her, and no obvious sign of a struggle."

"But she wasn't suicidal; I know that for sure," Regan said. "She said she was coming to my office right after she made a phone call. She said she had evidence that would prove Dr. Goatt, not Mireya, killed Martha. She was going to show it to me and then we were coming to see you."

"Do you know who was she calling before leaving?"

"Dr. Goatt."

Dave rolled his eyes, his artificial eye perfectly mimicking his good eye. "Now there's a great move to make. Call the person you think is a murderer and tell them you've got the goods on 'em. Smart."

"That's what I told her, but she insisted. It seemed safe enough, if you think about it, though. Make the call, leave home immediately, meet me, and then go to the police."

"This is what happens when civilians meddle" — Dave cast a hard look at Regan — "in what should be left to us."

Regan winced.

"Dave, that's a bit harsh, even if you're only teasing," Tom defended his wife.

"Who says I'm teasing? The only correct behavior from your wife is to say, 'Go to the police,' when someone starts in."

Color rose in Regan's cheeks. "Judi tried to do that, Dave. She called the police. She got shuttled off to you and you blew her off. That's when she turned to me."

Regan finished her statement with a challenging and purposeful bite into her chocolate-covered cookie.

"Both of you stop and take a deep breath," Tom instructed. "You both feel responsible for something you didn't — couldn't — prevent, and you're too good of friends to point fingers at one another."

Dave sipped his coffee and acquiesced.

"I'm sorry," Regan said.

"Dave, is Mireya Varner still in custody?" Tom asked.

"Yeah. She hasn't been charged yet and we've got until tomorrow sometime before her forty-eight hours are up and she has to be brought before a judge to get charged or released."

long as she could and fought him. Judi would at least have bloodied his hand and any other part of his anatomy she could reach. She might even have kicked over one of her pet urns before succumbing, scattering hard-to-clean-up ashes everywhere.

But there were no obvious signs of a struggle. It didn't make sense. At least it didn't if Dr. Goatt was the one who killed Judi. No, it seemed more reasonable to think Judi's killer was someone else, someone she would have let into her condo, someone who could have sedated her without Judi realizing what was happening, perhaps over a cup of coffee or tea. Dave's suggestion troubled her. Maybe Mireya did have an accomplice.

Still...Regan considered how Judi thought and how she said what she thought, no matter the consequences. Hadn't she said she wanted to watch Dr. Goatt twist? Could she have devised some sort of plan she believed would keep her safe while she confronted him?

Would she have invited her nemesis into her kitchen as she had Regan, told him to sit down, and then taunted him with what she'd done to ensure her safety before she showed him her evidence? Would Judi have been so foolish and so reckless as to say something like, "I've got you, I've told Regan McHenry everything, and if I don't turn up at her office in half-an-hour, you're toast!' Regan took a deep breath. She could almost hear Judi saying just that.

A thought occurred to Regan immediately, one she didn't particularly like. If Judi was right and Dr. Goatt was eliminating people who were a threat to him, Judi might have inadvertently added her name to his hit list.

She wished she could wait until the results of Judi's autopsy and the careful police inspection of Judi's condo were completed before taking the next step, but she knew autopsies took time, and if Dr. Goatt truly was a prime suspect, there was no time to waste.

Regan typed "William Goatt veterinarian" on her computer as soon as she got home. As she hoped, he had a practice as well as being on the SPCA list of vets. She wanted to have a look at him, his hands and face especially, as soon as possible.

The only problem was, since she'd had no trouble finding photos of Dr. Goatt online, if Judi had mentioned her name, he might have Googled Regan McHenry just as easily, and her webpage had her photograph on it. She couldn't turn up at his practice if he knew her face.

There was no way around it: Tom, using their cat, Harry, would have to become her eyes and ears. She was able to schedule a sick cat appointment with Dr. Goatt for the next morning at 9:00 a.m.

While she could count on Tom to do his part, Harry, whose ears perked up at the sound of his name being given on the phone, might take a little persuading. How was it that he seemed to know a trip to the vet was coming even when he only heard her side of the phone conversation and the cat carrier hadn't yet been taken out of the closet?

Regan had dinner ready and was waiting eagerly for Tom to come home after his 5 o'clock appointment. She hurried to the garage as soon as she heard the door being raised, and handed him a glass of wine before he was fully in the house.

"Uh-oh, wine in the garage," Tom laughed, "I hope this is medicinal after your misadventure today and not indicative of you having done something you shouldn't have." He kissed her on the cheek, "Or perhaps I should ask if the wine is to prepare me for something you plan to do."

"I haven't done anything and I don't intend to do anything. It's you who are going to do something."

He stretched out his response. "Oookaay."

"We've noticed Harry's been off his feed lately, haven't we? You're going to take him to see Dr. Goatt tomorrow morning."

"Has Harry been informed? You know how he loves to see the vet."

"Not yet, but he suspects something is up."

"And just why are Harry and I off on this taxing adventure?"

They had reached the kitchen by the time Regan answered. "I've been thinking about how Judi could have been killed. It doesn't make sense that she would have been a passive victim, especially not if the evil doctor killed her. I figure she would have fought her killer."

"Didn't Dave say there were no signs of a struggle?"

"He did, and that's a problem, but maybe Doctor Goatt cleaned up after he killed Judi. I want you to take a good look at him and see if you notice any signs of a struggle on him, you know, scratches or bruises or anything like that. I'd take Harry to him myself, but in this imagined scenario I've created, Judi may have mentioned my name to him, so I don't think it's a good idea."

Tom's forehead wrinkled as Regan spoke. "Do you think she did? Do you think you're in any danger?" There was tension in his voice as he questioned her.

"No," she shrugged dismissively, "I'd like to be proactive, is all." She didn't add just in case.

🏠🏠🏠🏠🏠🏠🏠🏠🏠🏠🏠

Harry, their large, gray cat, had once witnessed a murder. Regan rescued him after his owner was killed and they shared a special bond since she brought him home. He routinely allowed Regan to carry him like a baby, on his back with his paws folded over his body; that was his posture at 8:30 in the morning.

His relaxed pose changed as soon as he spotted the cat carrier. He didn't fight or scratch; he merely extended his extremities and held them rigid so his silhouette was larger than the opening to the carrier.

"Come on, Harry. You're just going to get a little checkup. It's no big deal."

Regan tried to angle him through the open door. Harry twisted and realigned his legs so he still didn't fit. He stared at her with accusing golden eyes.

"You know how you like to sit on my lap when I can't sleep at night because I'm trying to work something out. We're sleuthing partners. That's what we do. This isn't any different; you'll just be working with Tom instead of with me." Regan stroked his fur and offered encouragingly,

Regan frowned. 'Harry's already..."

"Exactly. Judi Pardini may have been right when she said he runs spay and neutering scams. But murder? I don't know, Sweetheart. After having met him, I just don't see him as a killer. Murdering two women because they were threatening to turn him in to the Veterinary Medical Board? Their charges might have been inconvenient for him, but you should see the awards and letters of appreciation he has plastered all over his waiting room walls. My guess is that their charges wouldn't be believed so murder to stop them seems like a real stretch to me."

🏠🏠🏠🏠🏠🏠🏠🏠🏠🏠🏠

Regan gave Dave plenty of time to get home from work, have dinner with Sandy, and have a beer or two before she called him. It had been five days since she discovered Judi's body and she hoped autopsy results and toxicology reports were in and that he might be in a talkative mood about them. If he wasn't, she had a good opening line to move him in that direction.

"You're not calling to see how my day went, are you?" Dave asked. "I can read you like a book. You want me to give you information about your pal, Judi Pardini, right?"

His questions called for yes or no answers. Instead of answering him, though, Regan responded like a politician with her own open-ended question. "What do you know that you think I'd want to know?"

"Autopsy and tox panel results on Judi Pardini," he answered with clipped precision.

Regan couldn't help but smile. The results were in and Dave had heard about them!

"Umm, that's doubtful. I don't think you'll have anything to tell me that I don't already know." She baited him and had fun doing it.

"Really? Fine. Let's change the subject."

He played his hand as well as she did. Better. Regan folded first.

"Aren't you even a little curious to know what I know?"

"You mean what you think you know," Dave taunted. "Sure, tell me."

Regan felt a flutter of triumph. She had just regained the upper hand in their game. She knew her friend as well as he knew her: he'd gleefully correct her logic mistakes. Once he did, she would get as much useful information by being wrong as by being right.

"Okay, first, Judi was murdered. I'd bet serious money that there was a small injection mark in her armpit just like there was on Martha."

"Figuring that out doesn't take much figuring," he said condescendingly.

"She was killed with insulin."

Dave made a yawning noise over the phone.

"I'll come back to the autopsy results in a minute, but I want to tell you what the Capitola police found when they did a careful sweep of Judi's condo, before we talk autopsy. There were no signs of forced entry and at first blush no signs of a struggle. But when they studied the area carefully, they found evidence that something untoward had happened in the kitchen." Regan had to bite her tongue to keep from adding, "didn't they" and giving it away that she was fishing.

"The kitchen had been cleaned up pretty well, but there was something — I don't know, something like a broken cup in the garbage or some sugar on the floor in a place where it didn't show until the police did a careful search, something — that changed their minds."

Dave cleared his throat and said nothing. He hadn't mocked her; that was big.

Emboldened, she tossed out her wild guess. "Getting back to the autopsy, there was a bit of skin found under her fingernails, wasn't there? Not much skin, nothing obvious, but it was there."

Dave remained silent while Regan's heart pounded. When he finally spoke, his tone held a mixture of dejection and betrayal.

"Who have you been talkin' to, Regan? You got a secret Capitola police buddy?"

"No, Dave. I haven't been talking to anyone." She tried to sound lighthearted. "You're my only mole."

"I swear...how did you know what was found? You psychic or something?"

Regan waited for his follow up mocking of her, but it didn't come.

"Am I right?" she asked incredulously.

"Right down to the material found under her fingernails."

"Whose skin was it?"

"Did I just hear your crystal ball crack? Don't you know whose skin it was?"

"Of course not. My guess would be Dr. Goatt — according to Tom, he has scratches on his hands that could have been inflicted by Judi as they struggled," she dropped her voice and hoped he wouldn't hear her, "or by one of his patients — but I was only imagining what might have happened. I don't have any real knowledge of what went on before Judi was murdered."

"I wish I had a recorder picking up what you just said, especially the part about imagining everything. Oh, boy. I'd play that over and over whenever I was havin' trouble falling asleep at night. Hearing you say you didn't know what you were talking about would make me feel all warm and cozy.

"FYI, because of your pal's accusations against him, we talked to good 'ole Billy Goatt right away. He's got a great alibi. He was performing spay and neutering operations the morning of Judi Pardini's murder and then he went to a lunch honoring him for his service at the SPCA. He was there accepting pats on the back until 2:00. Time of your pal Judi's death was placed at between 10:30 and 12:30 No need to go any further with him."

"Suppose he was making up the part about being in surgery."

"He had a helper."

"Suppose his helper lied. If Martha and Judi were right, he fabricated completed operations before. Maybe his assistant was in on it with him. Did the police think of that?"

"Suppose, suppose, suppose. You don't like it when you don't get your way."

"If not Dr. Goatt, who killed Martha and Judi?"

his feet and beg for mercy, but she said that wouldn't be helpful since he was quite clear about me having to leave.

"She reminded me how lucky I was having a few months to relocate. Then she said I'm to make my rent checks out to her and send them to her office. My life is crashing down and everything on her end is all tidy, and cold, and impersonal.

"I know you went to see her. I appreciate that. I guess it was too much to hope that you could find a saving loophole in my mother's contract."

"I never saw your mother's contract; Roya Matthews never showed it to me. She was under no obligation to do so and she wouldn't, citing probably correct ethical reasons for her decision.

"Judi said your mother had given her a copy of it to read. Unfortunately, when she told me that, she'd misplaced it. When I talked with her the morning she was killed, Judi said she had found the contract and, to be sure she didn't forget it, she would put it in the folder of evidence that she had about the veterinarian she and your mother thought was defrauding the SPCA.

"Judi was coming to my office later in the day. She was convinced the veterinarian had killed your mother to silence her and that he was coming after her, too. She thought the police had dismissed her as a batty old lady, but I have some sway with a good friend in the police department. Judi was going to bring the folder to my office and then we were going to take it to my friend and convince him the police needed to reconsider their opinion of Judi.

"The folder wasn't at her condo when the police did their crime scene search. That's one of the reasons I thought Judi was right about the veterinarian. It makes sense to me that he would have taken the folder and destroyed it to get rid of incriminating evidence after he killed Judi. But since the folder was never found, I never did get to see a copy of your mom's contract."

Mireya leaned toward Regan over the table. "The police never said anything to me about having another suspect. They just went on and on about how they knew I was guilty but hadn't yet put together a strong enough case to charge me."

"You were brought in for questioning during the time the police dismissed what Judi said about the veterinarian. Certainly, they didn't think he killed your mom. They had to start paying attention to him, though, when Judi was killed in the same way your mother was, and they couldn't make you a suspect because you were in custody. They've since ruled him out as Judi's killer because he has a strong alibi, but they also had to rule you out because you were in their custody at the time Judi was killed."

"Where did you get the idea they've given up on me? Haven't you heard? They think I got Jimmy to kill Judi, maybe even my mom, too. According to the police, they've just released me temporarily. They said I'll be rearrested and charged once they have enough evidence to arrest him and get him to 'flip on me'."

"You mentioned Jimmy before. Is he your boyfriend?"

"No. He's just a very sweet man who wishes he was. I love Jimmy, but not in that way, never in that way. I wish I could. Jimmy loves Jackson and would probably be a great dad to him, but much as I've tried, I just can't fall in love with him.

Regan spoke as gently as she could. "Martha didn't plan everything in her life, Mireya. She didn't plan to have a child out of wedlock, and she didn't intend for him to re-enter her life."

Regan watched emotions play across the young woman's face as Mireya fell silent for a good minute. When she spoke, her words were controlled and decisive. "I want to meet him. I need to meet him. I need to ask him what my mother said about me and Jackson. I need to know if she was so happy to have found him that she stopped caring about us."

"You know that's not true, Mireya. Your mother could never stop caring about you and Jackson. She might have opened her heart to her son, but she had a huge heart. She wouldn't have cut you and Jackson out of it to make room for him."

Tears streamed down Mireya's face. She made no attempt to wipe them away or to staunch them. She came close to screaming as she said, "I want to meet my brother!"

"I'm basing what I told you on surmise and second-hand information. We still don't know for sure that he's real, but even if he is, we don't know how to contact him. He's going to have to contact you."

"If I can't meet him, if you don't even know if what Judi said is true, why did you tell me about him? Why couldn't you let my mother take her secret to the grave with her?"

Their lunch orders arrived as orders always seem to: at the most inopportune time. As soon as the server placed the plate in front of her, Mireya shoved it away. She jumped up and ran out of the restaurant, leaving the server quite confused and Regan feeling terrible.

"Isn't this what she ordered?" the server entreated. "I can get her something else," he offered. "She didn't have to leave."

Tom found Regan sitting in front of her computer, eyes closed, head in hand, rubbing her forehead instead of working. He moved close to her, wordlessly tilted her head back against his stomach, and used his fingertips to gently massage her temples. "That bad?"

"Yes, that bad. That bad on multiple levels."

"You are the picture of a woman in serious need of a pizza and a glass of wine. You're going to come with me to the kitchen where I will use my fabulous culinary skills to open a bottle of a decent Sangiovese, pull a pizza out of the freezer and, picture this if you will," he rolled his hand with a magician's flourish, "set the oven to the proper temperature before inserting the pizza, and finally add cut tomatoes and cucumber to my famous 'bag-o-lettuce' green salad while you tell me all about the multiple levels of bad you experienced today."

"If that doesn't cheer me up, nothing will." Regan smiled weakly as she spoke, but she sounded miserable.

"My thoughts exactly," Tom said cheerily.

He pulled her up from her chair, took her by the hand, and walked them toward the kitchen. "Sit," he commanded when they reached their destination.

"Remember how I didn't want to tell Mireya about her brother?" Regan asked as Tom skillfully pulled the cork on the promised Sangiovese and shook his head, yes.

"Well, my telling elicited the same shock, upset, and confusion I imagined it might, together with the charge of my being an insensitive meddling clod to bring up the subject."

"Ouch," Tom said as he handed her a glass of wine.

"It was unpleasant, but I was prepared for that. What was worse, much worse, was the level of anger — almost hatred — Mireya expressed toward her mother. And then Mireya told me about a nice-sounding young man named Jimmy, who she said would do anything she asked, anything she even implied she wanted him to do, in his effort to make her fall in love with him.

"I can't shake the feeling that maybe he did something awful, thinking Mireya wanted him to, you know, like Henry II asking if there was no one who would rid him of that troublesome priest?

"Tom, suppose Mireya complained about Martha to him like she did to me? Or worse — and here's where my bad experiences take on a true mantle of horror — suppose Mireya asked him to do something to her mother?"

"Do you believe she's capable of that?"

"No," Regan answered quickly. "No, but I didn't expect her rancor," she said softly. "Mireya says the police think she and Jimmy planned Judi's death and killed her in a way that mimicked Martha's murder to give Mireya the perfect alibi."

"You think Mireya was willing to kill her mother because she was losing her house? And you think that she was willing to kill again to cover up her mother's murder? Those are pretty heady charges."

"And ones I don't believe." Regan's statement changed from certainty to hesitation as she went on, "But like Dave says, Mireya is a diabetic; she has access to insulin and knows how it works...Tom, I don't know what to think or what to do."

"If the police are investigating a conspiracy involving Mireya and her friend, or even if they think he acted alone, you know Dave is going to be up to his eyeball in the details of whatever's going on. Give him a call. Yes, he's going to give you a hard time, but after all your misadventures, you two seem to do that dance well. You can take whatever he throws at you, and after he's finished teasing you, he'll probably set your mind at ease."

"Or not."

"Either way, isn't that better than what you're imagining right now?"

Regan waited until well after dinner before she dialed Dave's number. The last time she called him late in the evening, she was fishing and thought she had the upper hand. Tonight was nothing like last time. She plastered a smile on her face as she dialed his number. Words coming through a smiling mouth always sounded more upbeat and tonight she needed all the positive energy she could muster.

"Hi, Dave, you want to do lunch tomorrow?"

"Can't. I have meetings from 10:00 till 3:00."

"I'm just taking some biscotti out of the oven." What she said wasn't true, of course — keep smiling she reminded herself — but she could easily make good on her fib. "Suppose I stop by on your morning coffee break with some."

"Nope. Doing an interview in the morning. Regan, I can tell you're trying to feed me and I know when you do that you think 'put food in him and out pops information.' Since we won't be getting together tomorrow, why don't you use that time to take a class on how to influence people using subtlety?"

She couldn't hold up the corners of her mouth any longer. "You're sort of right."

"Only sort of?"

"Yes, only sort of. I was calling because I may have information for you."

Dave groaned. "You mean you have one of your wild-goose-chasing ideas for me? And the fact that you said you 'may' have information for me instead of insisting I listen to your crazy imaginings means the goose you're about to toss in front of me is already half airborne".

"Stop it, Dave. I'm struggling here."

"Flap, flap, flap, there he goes."

Regan didn't offer a snappy comeback or defensive words.

"Aww-oh. You're serious," Dave declared.

"I'm afraid so."

"Spill."

"Is it true the police still think Mireya or her friend, Jimmy, killed Martha?"

"Yeah, we're still looking into something like that."

Regan could tell Dave had slipped into professional mode because he used "we" and inserted himself in the investigation.

"I had a troubling conversation with Mireya today. She told me Jimmy would do anything she asked him to do — sometimes even do things she didn't specifically ask him to do — in order to impress her. Do the police think that's what happened?"

Regan waited for a long time while Dave remained noncommittally quiet. "Or is it worse? Do the police really think Mireya orchestrated her mother's and Judi's killings?"

"Here's where you're going to tell me what you think you know. This is the information you may have for me, right?"

"That's my problem, Dave. I don't," Regan stammered, "can't…believe Mireya could do such a thing, but when we talked earlier today, she was so angry, so hurt. She blames her mother for the loss her house and her level of animosity…I don't know what I think anymore."

"Your little pal, Mireya, is still our prime suspect, but she's been playing the, 'I loved my Mommy so much' card real well that some of the team was kinda' havin' doubts about her. We professional law enforcement officers always rely on facts to make our case, not gossip, so your little conversation isn't going to hang your gal pal, Mireya. But when cops have doubts, sometimes details get overlooked, not on purpose, but that's just the way it goes, so what you told me is important, 'cause none of us have seen that side of her."

"I don't want to be right and I'm probably reading way too much into her behavior."

"Maybe. Maybe not. Thanks, Regan. Donuts are on me next time. I like that you're trying to be helpful while keeping out of trouble.

"Dave, wait, before you hang up, I've been so worried about what I saw today with Mireya and wondering if I should tell you — and how to tell you, I just realized there should be an easy way to rule out Jimmy. And if he's no longer a suspect, then doesn't that mean Mireya isn't either?"

Dave loudly let out a noise that fell halfway between a sign and a groan. "Here I thought I was gonna' get away with some useful info from you and no fuss. Why do I let myself hope? What did you have in mind?"

"You have skin, male skin, from under Judi's fingernails. Can't you get a DNA sample from Jimmy and compare the two?"

"You think we haven't thought of that? If good 'ole Jimmy doesn't want to give us a sample, well, courts are kind of particular about that, especially here in California. We can't force him to spit in a cup unless we charge him or have a search warrant for his DNA. So far, he's been keeping his mouth shut, literally, and so far, there's not any real evidence against him, so we're stuck.

"Besides, Jimmy's just our easiest Mireya-as-mommy-killer suspect. Even if Jimmy's not the murderer, it doesn't mean your gal pal couldn't have gotten some other guy to do the deed. But now — thanks to you — we know butter does melt in her mouth, so we'll be looking extra careful at her."

7

I've done it now, Regan thought. *I'm a gossip and a snitch.* She had repeated hearsay to Mireya with crushing results and then supplied Dave with a potential motive for murder that the already suspicious police might use against her. Could she have done more harm to the distraught young woman who thought she could count on Regan's friendship?

For the time being, at least, the guilt Regan felt outweighed any doubts she might have about Mireya's innocence in her mother's death. The least she could do, Regan decided, was reassure Mireya that her mother hadn't abandoned her. Then, since she had given the specter of him life, she could find Mireya's brother.

Regan knew she could easily do the first thing; but the second task, finding Mireya's illusory brother, well, she could only promise she would try.

Surely Martha hadn't upended Mireya's household to no end. She had purchased property in Carmel which Mireya would inherit. Even if it meant some disruption in her life, Mireya would no doubt do well as a result of her mother's real estate venture. County records would show the sale as

Regan immediately understood where Tom was going with his question. "Well, then, if Mireya is in custody, she couldn't have killed Judi, could she? If the Coroner finds insulin in Judi's body, that means whoever killed her, likely killed Martha, too, doesn't it? And that means Judi was right: Dr. Goatt must be guilty, doesn't it?"

Dave nodded gravely. "I see what you're asking. Same MO, but no opportunity. It sure looks like your pal Mireya didn't kill Judi Pardini." He paused. "Unless she has a helper that she told to do her dirty work"

"And as for your Dr. Goatt, we gotta see the evidence the Vic, if the coroner does rule her death a homicide, had on him.

"I got another question for you, though, Ms. Amateur Sleuth. There were no obvious signs of a struggle. So, if Mireya sent a hit man or if your Doctor Goatt killed her, how did Mireya's guy or 'ole Billy Goatt, the guy Judi Pardini thought was a murderer, get her to hold still while he injected her with insulin?"

Dave raised his eyebrows and took a huge bite out of his cupcake.

"Go. I'm shaken but I'll be fine. You have a five o'clock appointment."

"I can cancel it, Sweetheart."

"No. I'm all right. The chocolate did its job."

"Oh, good grief," Dave chimed in. "I can give her a ride home, Tom."

"Both of you, I'm fine," Regan said firmly. She was so convincingly insistent that she had recovered from finding Judi's body that at 4:45 she found herself alone in her car, driving home, her mind filled with questioning thoughts.

Dave had an excellent point about Dr. Goatt. She couldn't imagine Judi inviting him into her condo and then passively letting him kill her.

Even if he had somehow tricked her into opening her door to him, once he made a threatening move, Judi would have been screaming like Janet Leigh in *Psycho*, not resting quietly in her bed while he gave her a lethal injection. And if he had somehow forced his way into her living room and managed to sedate her, say by using a veterinary anesthesia in a hanky placed over her face, she would have held her breath for as

"There's a can of people tuna in your future if you cooperate."

Harry did nothing to earn his tuna treat, but after Regan managed to stuff him into the cat carrier, she decided she'd give it to him anyway as compensation for his traumatic morning.

"All ready, Harry?" Tom said as he picked up the cat carrier by its top handle. Harry protested mightily as he became airborne. "Wish us luck. We should be back in an hour."

Tom started to kiss Regan goodbye, and while she happily accepted his kiss, she changed her mind about sending them off on their way. "I'm coming with you," she announced.

"I thought you didn't want to risk being recognized."

"I don't. I'll stay in the car while you and Harry check out Dr. Goatt. That way you can tell me all about him while your impressions are fresh." She bent to Harry's level and spoke reassuringly to him, "See, Harry, you're on the case just like I said."

"You can't even wait twenty minutes for me to get home, can you?"

Regan smiled sheepishly as she grabbed her purse and an oversize scarf.

Regan drove. When Tom and Harry left her in the car, she wrapped the scarf up over her head and squished down in the driver's seat until anyone cursorily noticing her might assume she was an elderly Russian peasant woman driving a car that was too big for her. She wasn't good at sitting on the sidelines and she expressed her displeasure at having to do so by fidgeting and checking her watch every minute or two.

Her guys returned within twenty minutes, Tom smiling and Harry looking like he was going to need two cans of people tuna. His right front paw sported a tidy bandage.

"Complete debriefing on its way," Tom said as he put Harry in the back seat. "First, Dr. William Goatt matches his name surprisingly well. He's heavy-set...no, that's being too kind. He's grossly overweight and round from his hips to his neck, built with a long body and short arms and legs. He wears his hair kind of like Donald Trump does: long in the back and sort of swirled on each side." Tom waived his hands in circular motions on each side of his head for added clarity. "And he has a goatee. So between the hair, his build, and his facial hair, he really does resemble a goat standing on its hind legs."

Regan straightened up, removed her scarf and tossed it into the back seat next to Harry and backed out of her parking space. "The goatee is missing on his webpage photo," she said. "What about the important stuff?"

"He's scratched all over both hands. I asked him about his wounds and he said they were occupational hazards. I had to believe him because Harry scratched him during the examination."

"Harry scratched him? Harry doesn't behave like that." Regan defended her cat.

"He did today. I'd say Harry didn't like Dr. Goatt much at all. It could be because the doctor suggested a blood panel for him — that's why the bandage — and suggested Harry should be neutered," Tom laughed.

"We don't know yet. I can tell you this much, though. The skin belonged to a male suspect whose DNA isn't in the criminal database of CODIS."

"Again in English please," Regan requested.

Dave spoke with exaggerated slowness. "We ran the DNA recovered at the crime scene against the Offenders Database at the Combined DNA Index System, CODIS. That's the national database for convicted US criminals. We didn't get any hits. That means whoever the guy is who killed Judi isn't a convicted felon."

"Dr. Goatt isn't a convicted felon."

"Neither is Tom, or me, or most men. It's time to move on, Regan, before your obsession about 'ole Dr. Billy Goatt butts you in the bum."

6

Regan joined Tom on the patio, coffee cup in hand. Her only offer of conversation was a stage-worth sigh.

"The sun's out. It's your day off. Why do you seem so morose?" he asked.

"My scruples tell me I have to tell Mireya what Judi told me about her having a half-brother, but every other part of my body and soul are screaming, 'No, no, no.' Let someone else do it."

"Is there anyone else who knows what you do?"

"That's the problem. I don't think there is. I'm not even sure the half-brother knows. Martha may have been planning to surprise him with Mireya just like she was going to surprise Mireya with him. Can't I just pretend Judi never told me anything?" Regan pleaded, knowing the answer Tom would give her.

"Sorry, Sweetheart. It sounds like you have no choice," he said sympathetically.

"I've invited Mireya to lunch at Laili — I figured, if I have to do it, I may as well break the news in as pleasant a place as possible and I used the pretext of celebrating her release from police custody as an excuse to get together — but even the prospect of lunch at one of my favorite restaurants isn't making me feel better."

"Maybe she'll be happy. Her parents are both dead now; a brother would be family for her. Didn't you say she's feeling like her mother did something terrible to her by changing her will? Maybe if Mireya understands why, it will help her."

"You're the best husband. You always try to cheer me up, don't you?"

"I do my best. And yes, I am the best husband in Santa Cruz County, maybe in California," he said with great earnestness and a big smile on his face.

⌂ ⌂ ⌂ ⌂ ⌂ ⌂ ⌂ ⌂ ⌂ ⌂ ⌂

"Thank you for taking me to lunch on one of the worst weeks of my life," an unsmiling Mireya said as she slipped into a chair in the garden courtyard at Laili. "This is — was — one of Mom's favorite restaurants."

Regan offered a subdued smile. "It's one of my favorites, too, and hopefully you'll enjoy eating here."

She didn't expect the reaction her words brought; Mireya jumped up and hugged her. "There's nothing like being taken into custody and implicated in your mother's murder to let you see who your real friends are. In a place like Santa Cruz, where you can't go anywhere without running into half a dozen people you know, I'm so pleased you're willing to be seen in public with me and at one of your favorite places, too. Most of the people I thought I could count on wouldn't be."

Mireya released Regan and returned to her seat. "You'd be amazed how many of them won't even talk to me," she said bitterly. "I thought I'd have to be convicted of something before shunning began, but I guess I'm notorious now and that's enough for many of them."

Regan reached across the table and patted her luncheon guest's hand. "Hold your head up high, Mireya. They'll feel differently when your mother's murder is solved. You'll see. They'll be your friends again," she soothed.

"I don't want them back as friends, not if they were so willing to believe that I could kill my own mom. There's nothing keeping me here now. When this is over, I'm going to take Jackson and make a new home somewhere else."

"Surely not everyone has turned their back on you?"

"Well, you haven't. And Mrs. Ortzi, the lovely woman who takes care of Jackson for me when I'm at work, hasn't. And, of course, Jimmy, my dear, wonderful, friend Jimmy, hasn't. but," Mireya pressed her hand against her nose and sniffed, trying to stem tears that were ready to fall, "I feel so alone and abandoned."

Regan opened her mouth, ready to tell Mireya that she wasn't as alone as she thought, but Mireya went on and Regan was relieved that she could hold off a little longer and think some more about just how she should bring up Mireya's new family member.

"I got a call from that Carmel real estate agent this morning. Escrow is closing in two more days. She's going to be the property manager for her client until I leave and then she's going to list my house. I asked if she would tell me who her client was and where he lived so I could throw myself at

"I watched my parents and saw the marriage they had. I want that kind of relationship, that kind of two-people-in-love thing that should be part of marriage. I won't settle. I didn't settle for Jackson's dad because I saw his weaknesses and realized what marriage to him would be like."

Mireya rolled her eyes and chuckled. "I don't know why his flaws weren't apparent to me before Jackson was conceived — not that I regret having had my wonderful little boy — but they weren't. I guess I was too immature and too much in lust to notice them.

"But now, even if it would be good for Jackson, I can't settle for Jimmy. Poor Jimmy keeps trying so hard to win my heart. All I have to do is mention a need or a wish that I have and he takes care of it or makes it happen. Everything he does is in vain, though. I'll wait as long as I have to for the right person."

The lull in the conversation meant Regan had to speak. "Mireya, Judi told me something your mother told her in secret, something important in your mother's past. It may have been the surprise your mother was going to share with you in Carmel."

"You mean her surprise was something more than that my 'loving mother' was arranging to throw Jackson and me out of our house?" There was so much anger and bitterness in Mireya's question that it startled Regan.

"According to Judi, your mother told her that you weren't an only child." The second the words left her mouth, Regan wished she had let the harshness of Mireya's question settle for a minute and softened her announcement. Unfortunately, she hadn't, and now she couldn't take her words back.

Mireya shook her head, a blank look on her face. "What are you saying, Regan. My parent's only had me, and I was… they had a hard time conceiving me."

"Your mother told Judi that she gave birth to a son well before she met your father and that she put him up for adoption." Regan waited for Mireya to assimilate what she just said.

"But she never said anything…"

"I think that she was going to tell you her history at lunch. There's more, Mireya. According to Judi, your mother recently reconnected with him at an SPCA fundraiser in Carmel. It sounds like he lives nearby. My guess would be that, if he's real, he lives in or near Carmel.

"Judi said your mother told her he has a dog like Queeny, but that's all the information we have about him at this point. I believe your mother was selling her house to buy something in Carmel so she could be close to him."

"And she sold my house, too, to do this?" Mireya's voice rose an octave during her short question.

"I'm still not certain that she intended for your house to be part of the deal, and I can't tell without seeing the contract. She may have used it as collateral for part of her down payment, thinking she could put a mortgage on it if she needed to come up with more cash. The sale of your house being forced may have just happened with her death."

"My mother planned her whole life with great care," Mireya said, becoming more agitated with every word. "She wouldn't have done what she did if she didn't intend for my house to be part of the sale."

soon as escrow closed, and while Mireya might not be able to do anything with the property until Martha's estate was settled, in the meantime Regan could take a look at the property Martha purchased and assure Mireya that she and Jackson would be fine.

To find out about Martha's purchase, Regan could wait until Martha's estate was settled and get information from her attorney, she could wait a month until sales records were available online, she could go directly to the Recorder's Office for Monterey County in Salinas and look it up, or she could try one more time to get Roya Matthews to show her a copy of Martha's purchase contract.

Patience was not a virtue Regan had mastered. She ruled out her first two options and decided on a visit to the Salinas Recorder's Office via a round-about route through Carmel. If Roya agreed that, with escrow closed, there was no longer a reason for confidentiality and co-operated, she wouldn't have to travel farther.

Regan considered asking Tom if he wanted to make a day of it, but remembered his comment about what an attractive woman Roya Matthews was. Although she didn't consider herself given to jealousy, she wrinkled her nose in reflection and decided she'd make a solo trip. And she'd go dressed in her finest skirmish clothing. Let Roya be golden; she'd be her equal in red and black.

Regan had debated doing a pop-in, but decided against it and had made an appointment to meet with Roya Matthews. When she arrived, she was escorted to Roya's office to be greeted by an again metallic-clothed woman on her feet standing behind her desk with her hand extended across it in greeting. Her outfit du jour had hints of copper in it, although it was still predominantly golden.

Regan was aware Roya was tall after their first meeting, but today she was taller than Regan, a surprise because Regan was wearing three-inch stilettos which boosted her five-feet nine stance to a full six feet. Had Roya anted-up the heel height by adding platforms to the bottom of her shoes? With the desk between them, a thwarted Regan couldn't tell.

Roya smiled warmly through coral lipstick that matched perfectly the subtle floral design on her signature scarf. "Please have a seat and promise me you won't ask me for a copy of Martha Varner's purchase contract again," Roya trilled.

"Oh dear. That's exactly what I intended to do," Regan countered, smiling to match Roya's mien.

"Hum, well this may be a short meeting, then." Roya kept a smile on her face, but the tone of her voice indicated it was an effort for her to do so.

"Escrow has closed; do you still consider the contract a private matter?"

"Not a private matter entirely. Just a bit of business that doesn't concern you at all. I don't understand, Regan. Why are you so insistent in insinuating yourself in my transaction?" Roya's lips had turned from smiling to a decidedly straight line.

Regan sighed and shrugged her shoulders. "You know how it is in this business: some clients become true friends. Martha was one of those; I really enjoyed knowing her. I didn't have the same connection with Mireya, but she came to me when she needed help. I feel a sense of responsibility to her, but more importantly to Martha. I know how much Martha loved her daughter, so anything I can do to help Mireya seems like a way of honoring Martha's memory."

As Regan explained her feelings, Roya's countenance hardened ever so slightly. It was a subtle transformation, but Regan was good at reading people and it didn't escape her notice.

"I must meet that little prima donna sometime," Roya said. "Her ability to get people to do her bidding is amazing. As for making clients into friends, that seems to be a behavior we don't share. I have plenty of useful clients whose backs I scratch and who scratch mine in return, but I'm primarily a businesswoman, Regan, so when I want to make friends, I don't look for candidates amid my client lists."

"Oh, well, we each have our own style, don't we? You probably wait around until your 'friends' send business your way and get warm fuzzy feelings when they do. I prefer a superior advertising campaign and involvement with the right charities to generate my clients."

Regan wondered if Roya was as good at reading body language and facial expressions as she was because, if Roya was, she'd know Regan wasn't impressed by her "style."

"No point in wasting anymore of your time — or mine — Roya. I'll be on my way." Regan took some modest satisfaction from the fact that she had ended their encounter before the tarnished golden girl dismissed her. Her only regret was that she hadn't asked Tom to come with her. Even if he still considered her an attractive woman, he would no longer be any more impressed with Roya Matthews than she was.

Regan arrived at the Salinas Recorder's Office feeling overdressed and incredibly tall. The Salinas employees dressed like their counterparts in Santa Cruz: like they might head outside during a lunch break and sit cross-legged on the grass. She unbuttoned her jacket and slouched at the counter so she could rest her elbows on it.

"Hi. I'd like to find out the location of a property a friend of mine just bought. It's in Carmel."

The employee didn't raise her eyes from her computer screen. "What's the name of the purchaser?" she asked in a bored monotone.

"Varner, Martha Varner."

"I'm not seeing anything. When did she purchase the property?"

"Escrow closed yesterday."

The employee didn't move anything more than her gaze, which she rotated to look up at Regan. "Why didn't you say it was an extremely recent purchase?"

Regan thought she detected a slight emphasis on the word extremely, but she couldn't be sure and decided she may only have imagined it.

"You have a great deal of confidence in our efficiency here, don't you?" the employee asked in pancake-flat fashion. "Hum. I guess it's not misplaced. Here it is in today's entry file, which hasn't even been loaded to the permanent record yet."

Regan wanted to yell "Yippy" but didn't dare break the solemnity of the employee's discovery.

"There's a five-dollar fee for a printout of the record and details if you want a copy."

Regan fished in her purse, found her wallet and produced exact change.

"You can pick up your paperwork at the first printer on your left." The employee inclined her head an inch in the direction she indicated before returning her eyes to the computer in front of her.

Regan picked up the single page printout and read it. There was a property address and a purchase price, but no details about the house on it. She was accustomed to seeing square footage, number of bedrooms and bathrooms, and sometimes quite a bit more information on corresponding printouts from Santa Cruz.

"Excuse me," she returned to the counter and the bored employee. "I think your computer jammed. I only got the first page of the printout. It just states the property address."

"That's all there is."

"Am I here too soon? Will more information be entered later?"

"That's all the information there is. I recognize the address. It's in Rancho Granada Village. You can tell your friend good luck with her purchase. That development has been tied up with protests and Supervisors for a decade. Last I heard it was finally approved, but within a few weeks there was a challenge filed in court. It's probably going to be another decade before anything gets settled."

"What does that mean?" Regan furrowed her brow.

"What do you think it means?" the bored employee stated before she dropped her eyes to her computer screen and began tapping on her keyboard, signaling their conversation had come to an end.

As soon as Regan got into her car, she posted Martha's newly purchased address into her GPS system and was rewarded with a map. She breathed a sigh of relief. If there was a map to the address, the barely animated computer addicted employee must have been mistaken.

She wanted as much information as possible to take back to Mireya about what could become her new home. Since the sale was complete, the house would be empty and any alarm system likely disabled, waiting for its new occupant to set up their preferences. She could stop by, peek in some windows, jiggle a few doors, and if need be, encourage a door to unlock without much concern that authorities would be alerted. If a neighbor caught her, she already had an excuse in her mind for what she was doing, and given her outfit, complete with stiletto heels, she was sure she could sell it because she hardly looked the part of a burglar.

GPS led her up Carmel Valley Road past the shopping centers at its base and by the Quail Lodge and Golf Course. The road climbed and narrowed slightly, but there were still broad low-lying expanses of land, especially on the right side of the road. *Turn left in ½ mile,* her GPS instructed. As she approached and her GPS counted down the distance, Regan noticed a marker constructed of golden Carmel stone, the signature building material of the area. It had fanciful wrought iron lettering on it which read, "Welcome to Rancho Granada Village."

Regan smiled and put on her blinker. Nothing was visible from the entry except a perfectly paved road which wound uphill, promising some of the properties would have ocean peeks or views. Since Martha had lived with an ocean view from her Capitola condo for so many years, Regan was willing to bet Martha's new house was in an elevated location and had one, too.

Narrow paved streets began branching off the main entry road after half a mile. She didn't see homes, but her GPS told her Martha's purchase was still another three-quarters of a mile up the hill and, therefore, still hidden from view. Regan continued her climb.

Turn right in 400 yards at Casitas Road the GPS instructed. As she made the turn where the wrought iron writing on another Carmel stone marker announced Casitas Road, Regan began to worry. The landscape was still devoid of structures.

The GPS counted down distances and finally announced *You have reached your destination*. Regan got out of her car. A soft breeze wafted through her hair as she turned around slowly until she had completed a three-hundred-and-sixty-degree rotation. Yes, there was an ocean view — a decent one — but outside of that feature, she stood overlooking the occasional Coastal Live Oak and scrubby manzanita and toyon bushes growing forlornly amid a desolate landscape which was scarred irregularly by the black serpentine pavement of small lanes. A modestly sized Carmel stone marker had the address number of Martha's purchase on it, but rather than announcing a grand house or a quintessentially charming and cozy Carmel home, the foreboding barrenness surrounding it made it seem more like a grave marker than a Welcome Home signpost.

Regan reread the single page printout she brought with her from the Salinas Recorder's Office. There must be some mistake. It indicated Martha had paid $1,900,000 for her barren plot of land, more than the value of her condo and Mireya's house combined. Regan knew Martha was comfortable in her retirement, but she wasn't a rich woman. Even with the two properties values included against the purchase price, she likely had needed to liquidate many, if not all, of her other assets to complete the purchase. What was she thinking?

Mireya would be devastated. *How can I tell her what her mother did?* Regan wondered. She got back in her car and descended toward the Rancho Granada Village turnout. As she approached the Carmel stone marker, she noticed there was a clear plastic box affixed to its back.

She stopped her car, not worrying that she left it in the middle of the roadway, and walked to the stand. As she tugged on the handle of the framed plastic door to open it, her heart began to pound rapidly. Smiling out at her was a likeness she recognized: Roya Matthews, appearing more golden than the Carmel stone behind her. Reagan reached inside the container and retrieved a flyer. It unfolded to reveal a map of the yet-to-be-developed Village and a boldly printed invitation to contact Roya Matthews to find out how to become a member of the fabulous community of Rancho Grande Village.

Regan didn't trust herself to talk and drive at the same time, so she refrained from using her hands-free phone. She even worried that she shouldn't think about her newly discovered information and drive at the same time, so she tried to put her visit to Rancho Grande Village out of her mind as she made her way back to Santa Cruz. It was an impossible undertaking but, although one irate driver beeped at her when she missed a red light turning green, she managed to drive safely back to Santa Cruz.

She pulled into the Kiley and Associates parking lot and saw Tom's car parked there. She couldn't wait to see him and tell him about Roya Matthews connection to Martha Varner's purchase. She practically flew down the hall to his office, but when she got there, his door was open and he was nowhere in sight.

Regan continued forward to the reception area. "Amanda, where's Tom?" she asked urgently.

"You just missed him. He went out with a client to look at some land they wanted him to see."

More land. Empty land. It was a day for homeless land. Regan felt her vexation level rising. What Roya Matthews had done to Martha Varner was not illegal — real estate agents and brokers could represent both buyers and sellers at the same time if they performed their fiduciary duty to both clients. But given the price of Martha's parcel…Regan fumed alone without Tom to steady her.

She recalled the comment made by the employee in the Salinas Recorder's Office and determined to do some research while she waited for Tom's return. She Googled Rancho Grande Village. The articles she found took her from annoyed to outraged. Development of the project looked great on paper, but it had been stalled by public outcry, forced to downsize, and just when it seemed like the development was about to clear all the red tape Monterey County had wrapped around it, a court challenge had been mounted which threatened to, like the Recorder's Office employee said, add another decade to getting final approval for the project before Martha could do anything with her parcel.

As Regan noted the date the court proceedings had been filed, she realized the contract Martha Varner had entered into probably happened after that date. If that was the case, there was a strong argument that Roya Matthews' fiduciary duty to Martha had been overwhelmed by her interest on behalf of the seller. Representing both sides of a transaction was always tricky, but favoring one side over the other so blatantly could get a real estate agent in trouble. She needed to see the contract.

Her cell phone twanged in her purse. Regan retrieved it and checked her caller ID. It was Dave.

"I thought you'd want to know, since you've been playing mother hen to Mireya Varner, that her pal, Jimmy, finally agreed to give us a DNA sample. Negative."

The news Dave was telling her should have been delivered contritely since, thanks to her, he had once again become suspicious of Mireya, but it sounded like a gloat rather than a confession.

"So that means Mireya is in the clear, then, doesn't it?"

"Ooh, this is too easy," his words came out like the lyrics to a jubilant song. "I really didn't think you'd jump to clearing your little gal pal that quickly. I thought I'd have to do a little more setup, a little more work to get you to ask that question," he warbled on with clear glee. "No, it doesn't. You want to know why?"

"Does it matter? You're going to tell regardless of what I say."

"Okay. You got one thing right today. You got the answer to that question right."

She could imagine his smile growing to a full half-moon shape as he continued.

"It seems three days before her mom was killed, Mireya drained her savings to the tune of seventy-five-hundred dollars. Yep, practically cleaned out her account. Got the money in cash. Naturally, when we found that out, we called her in and had a little talk with her about her spending habits. We tried real hard to help her explain where the money went, you know, maybe she bought a sweet little used car, we asked, or a little boat. Maybe she bought a diamond bracelet she saw in a store window and just had to have. But mums-the-word from her.

"So you know what we're thinking? We're thinking a Jimmy who isn't Jimmy. We're thinking a hit man."

"Surely there's another explanation."

"Yeah, you'd think so, but since she won't tell us what she did with the money or why she needed it in cash, we're kind of stuck with the hit man idea. She hasn't been charged yet, but we're closer than we've ever been."

"Dave, how can you say that? There's nothing real to connect Mireya with her mother's death."

"Nothin' but access to and understanding of the unusual murder weapon, a motive of anger aimed at her mother, and a missing bunch of cash that she spent mysteriously."

"That's all circumstantial. No, not even circumstantial; what you have could more accurately be described as coincidental."

"Which is why your little gal buddy is still free to go to the movies rather than sitting in a jail cell. We haven't made a good enough case, yet. Not yet, Regan, but we will. Well," he warbled happily, "I've got to go. You have a nice rest of the day."

"Dave! Dave?" He was gone and she was left unnerved. Roya Matthews' possibly unethical behavior was erased from her mind while she focused on the more pressing issue of what to do about Mireya. If only she didn't have her doubts about her even before Dave's call.

When faced with a problem, Regan was quick to tackle it. That was her personal modus operandi. She'd have to put aside feeling guilty about sharing her impressions of the young woman with Dave for the time being, and she'd have to apologize to Mireya for the way she handled bringing up her half-brother at their lunch, but she needed to call Mireya.

Regan picked up her phone and dialed Mireya's number. The call went to Mireya's answering machine, but as Regan began to leave her message, Mireya picked up.

"Regan, it's so good to hear a friendly voice." Mireya's sounded exhausted, but there was no mention of tension between them after Regan's revelation. "I'm screening all my calls just to make sure I don't respond if the police call. They might, too, because they're hassling me again even though I talked Jimmy into giving them a DNA sample and they ruled him out as a suspect."

She sighed deeply, echoing palpable self-reproach. "Poor dear man. I actually began to question whether or not he had done something awful, thinking I might want him to. I was so relieved to hear he's been cleared, and so ashamed to have doubted him."

Regan knew exactly how Mireya felt, except that she was still in the midst of doubt, still feeling guilty for being there, and still uncertain of the outcome of her suspicions.

"Now the police have a new theory." Mireya's words trailed off to a whimper. "They think I hired someone to kill Mom."

A suspect in Regan's mind or not, she heard so much pain in Mireya's voice, she had to see her. "Mireya, are you at home? Can I come over?"

"Would you?" Mireya pleaded. "I think I'm in serious trouble because of what I've done and I need to tell someone I trust about it. Jackson just went down for his nap so now's a good time. Is it a good time for you?" she entreated hopefully.

"I can be there in ten minutes."

"Thank you. Thank you so much."

Mireya's house was only about a half-hour's brisk walk from Regan's office, and on a normal sunny even if somewhat blustery day when she had already spent so much time in the car, she would have gone there on foot, but since she promised she'd be there in ten minutes, she took her car.

Mireya's front door opened as soon as she pulled to the curb in front of the house. The young woman was standing in the doorway as Regan approached, her arms wrapped tightly around herself, appearing smaller in stature than normal, waiflike, and miserable. Her eyes were red-rimmed and she chewed on her lower lip.

The two women wordlessly hugged at the door and then Regan intuitively moved into the living room uninvited. She decided to speak first and pointedly.

"I've talked to my friend Officer Dave Everett, so I know the police found you had made a sizable withdrawal from your savings account. He said you were unwilling to tell them what you used the money for, which is why they're suspicious of you, especially since their minds run to conspiracies and paid-for-hire killers."

Regan watched carefully to see Mireya's reaction to her words. There was none. Mireya didn't object to anything she said and didn't try to defend her actions or offer an explanation for them.

"Mireya, what's going on?"

Mireya flopped down on her sofa and put a hand on the seat cushion on either side of her. She kept arms rigid and held her head slightly down, the tension in her body clearly visible. Then she raised her chin and gazed up at Regan through moist eyelashes.

Regan sat down next to her. "Tell me, Mireya."

"I've done something stupid that's going to look really bad and I don't know how to make it better. If I tell you everything, is it like attorney-client privilege because you're my realtor?"

"No, Mireya, it doesn't work that way. I am your friend, though, and will try to help you in any way I can."

"At least promise me you won't tell the police what I tell you."

Regan took a deep breath. "I don't think I can make that promise. But I do think you'll feel better after you tell me what you've done."

Mireya nodded quickly. "You remember I told you I knew Jackson's father had problems?"

"I remember."

"Well, his flaws weren't just that he was immature or unreliable. He was a felon. He'd been convicted of armed robbery when he was nineteen and done three years in prison. He always said he got in with a bad crowd and had changed and grown up and wasn't about to do anything like that ever again. I wanted to believe him because I thought I loved him, so I did.

"But when I got pregnant with Jackson, he disappeared. Really grown up, really changed I figured. I assumed he ran back to Vancouver where he was from and decided, with my mom's help I'd be fine without him, that I'd probably be better off without him. My mom jumped in with both feet to help me financially, emotionally, and in every way she possibly could. She seemed terrified that I'd terminate my pregnancy or give Jackson away after he was born.

"Of course, I wasn't about to do either of those things, but even after I promised her I wouldn't, she still always seemed so worried. The expression she'd get on her face any time I'd complain about the slightest thing when I was pregnant was absolutely unnerving. She'd make me promise again and again that I'd keep my baby, and when she found out during an ultrasound that he was a boy, everything with her seemed to escalate."

Poor Martha, Regan thought. Judi was right about her fearing her daughter would give away her baby like she had done.

Mireya spoke softly. "I understand what she was going through now, since you told me about my mother's past. I wish she had told me about it herself. I can't imagine not being able to hold Jackson in my arms. She must have missed her son so much.

"Hunter, that's Jackson's father, turned up about a week before my mother was...died. He said that he hadn't run away, just panicked when I told him I was pregnant and gone back home to figure things out.

"He said he came back for me, for us, within a month, but that my mom intercepted him before he could see me. According to Hunter, she laid this huge guilt trip on him about his past and told him he needed to prove himself before he was worthy of being part of my life. I guess he was pretty terrified of being a dad anyway, so when she offered him a thousand dollars a month to go back to Canada and leave us alone, he agreed."

Regan put her arm around Mireya and pulled her close.

"You see how it will look when the police find that out? They'll say when I found out my mom paid my baby's father to get out of our lives, I was so angry at her that I wanted her dead. And that's before I found out she was about to force me out of my house. Can you imagine what they'll make of that when they put both things together?"

Unfortunately, Regan could.

"And it gets worse, Regan, much worse. Hunter said he had been saving all the money my mother gave him and that he was ready to buy us a little house in Canada, not in Vancouver because it's very expensive there, but in an area about an hour's drive further inland. He said he was close to having enough money to do it but that he just needed a little more. He said he wanted, expected, Jackson and me to move there with him. He said he had a good job and had really changed and that more than anything he wanted the opportunity to be a good father to Jackson.

"When I told him I didn't want to move to Canada, he got really quiet and said he was serious about being a dad and that his own dad died recently and his mom was devastated. He said he wanted her to have a chance to be close to the grandson she had never seen because he was sure that would make her life better. Then he said he didn't want to, but that if I wouldn't cooperate, he would demand his rights and force a custody battle. Even though I was pretty sure he wouldn't win one, I felt like I couldn't take the chance. I was terrified I might lose Jackson.

"I thought, hoped I guess, that what he was really doing was cleverly asking for more money and not going after Jackson, so I told him I'd see if between us Mom and I could come up with an increase in his monthly payments if he'd just go back to Canada. Hunter blew up. He said he never expected I'd try to buy him off, too. He yelled 'Like mother like daughter' at me and said all this time he had been putting his life back together because he loved me and thought I loved him, and that if he just did what my mother wanted and proved he had changed, we could be a family.

"I felt terrible about what I'd suggested, but just when I was about to throw my arms around him, tell him I did still care, and apologize for doubting him, he said that my plan would never have worked anyway because my mom sent him a letter saying she was out of money and wouldn't be paying him off anymore. As soon as he said that, I figured I was right about him asking for money after all.

"I told him I'd give him seventy-five hundred dollars, all the money I had, if he'd leave us alone. He just shook his head and said, 'Sure. I can use the money.' So I went to my bank that same day, took out cash, and gave it to him. When I handed him the money, all he said was that he'd settle up with me and my mother soon enough. Then he kissed me on the forehead and left.

"So now the police think I paid him to kill my mother and I wonder if he did, if that's what he meant about settling up, and if he might try to settle up with me next. Regan, what am I going to do?"

"You won't like my answer, Mireya. What you're going to do is get Jackson settled — maybe the woman who watches him when you're at work take him in full time — and tell the whole story to the police."

"But they'll arrest me," Mireya squeaked.

"They probably will, temporarily, but if Hunter intends to harm you, at least you'll be safe in custody. And while you are, they'll find him and question him. If they charge him, they'll test his DNA so, if he killed your mother, we'll know."

"But what about me? If he did, they'll say I paid him to do it."

If she was confident in Mireya's innocence, Regan might have mumbled some reassuring platitude about justice being done and innocence winning out, but even after hearing Mireya's account, she was still conflicted. What Mireya said, the way she said it, seemed so honest, but Regan, who prided herself on being a pretty good judge of character, knew she was sometimes wrong about people, especially people who had a great stake in the lies they told. She was wary and not completely sure she should believe Mireya.

"Will Hunter's story be the same as yours?"

"It will be if he tells the truth, but I don't know if he will because at this point, I don't know if he loves me or hates me."

"You really have no choice but to go to the police, Mireya. I'll go with you if you want."

"What about your friend who's a policeman?"

"Dave?"

"Yes. Can't you explain what happened to him and ask him to back off?"

"My friendship with him doesn't work like that, and even if it did, it's the police who are actively investigating you, not him. You have a better chance of being believed and moving the investigation if you step up first than you do if they figure out your Hunter connection and try to make up their own story about what happened."

A single tear ran down Mireya's cheek. "I know you're right. I'll make arrangements with Mrs. Ortzi and drop

Jackson off as soon as he wakes up. I'll go to the police today."

"Do you want me to come with you?" Regan asked again.

"No. I have to do this on my own."

8

Regan waited until midday to call Dave. "Is Mireya Varner in custody?" she asked when he answered his phone.

"Nope."

Regan took a deep breath. "Well, that's a relief. That must mean the police believe her. I am a little worried about her safety, though, in case Hunter comes after her. Is she being protected?"

"What are you talking about, Regan? Sounds like once again you're off in some little world I don't know anything about."

"You must be slipping. I thought you stayed on top of everything that happens at the SCPD. Didn't you know Mireya came in last night to explain why she took money out of her bank account?"

"Nope. And I'm not slipping. She hasn't come by for a little chat."

"But, when I spoke with her yesterday, she said she would as soon as she got her son settled."

"Can you say liar, liar, pants on fire about a woman or does that only apply to a guy? She hasn't graced Santa Cruz's finest with her presence."

Regan badly wanted to give Mireya the benefit of doubt — perhaps she was having trouble finding care for Jackson — but it was hard. "Dave, we better talk. Can I come by your office?"

"I think you should. Half-a-hour enough time for you to get here?"

"Yes," she answered simply.

Regan stopped by Mireya's house on her way to see Dave. Originally, she planned to upbraid Mireya for taking so long to go to the police and tell her she was on her way there with or without her young former client, but by the time she reached Mireya's front door, she had moved beyond faulting the young woman to worrying about her.

Suppose something had happened to her? Suppose Mireya's fears about Hunter settling things with her in a violent way were valid? Suppose Mireya was lying dead in her house…she reined in her wild thoughts and knocked on the front door. She rapped again quickly and rang the doorbell for good measure. There was no answer. The entry door had an insert of leaded glass at it's top. Regan was tall, but even though she stood on tip-toes and then tried jumping up and up and down a couple of times, she couldn't see in through it.

Regan left the porch and walked around the house, peering in the dining room window as she passed it, and saw nothing but an empty room. She took the two steps up to the raised deck at the back of the house and reached the French doors that opened to the kitchen and knocked there. Still no answer or movement in the house. She twisted the door handle; it was locked. Her heart rate picked up and her imagination raced. Was Mireya lying dead in her home just out of her view?

Regan had on occasion poked around in an empty house when she shouldn't have, but she had always used a lockbox to gain entrance, never broken in. French doors, especially older ones like the doors on Mireya's house, were notoriously ill fitting and therefore somewhat flexible and she had heard credit cards were useful in encouraging locks to give up their guard duties. Regan peered left and right and over her shoulder guiltily as she pulled her wallet out of her purse and selected, not a credit card, but a library card made of similarly hard plastic. She squeezed it between the doors just below the handle and slid it up toward the hardware. She jumped when the pop she heard signaled her first attempt at being a cat burglar was successful. This time, when she twisted the handle, the door opened.

Regan's first step into the kitchen was tentative. She still held the handle and kept one foot on the deck as she called out, "Mireya?" She stepped inside fully and raised her voice. "Mireya?"

She moved from the kitchen to the dining room and walked through it to the living room, searching as she moved. She walked out of the living room into the entry hall at the front door and then turned and started down the hall that ran down the right side of the house as a corridor between first Jackson's bedroom, the single bathroom in the house, and finally Mireya's bedroom at the back of the house.

She peered into each new room with her shoulders up and her eyes almost squinting, prepared for the worst, but when she finished her search by rounding the far side of Mireya's bed without discovering anything she feared seeing, her attitude changed from fearful to perturbed.

She noticed there was a clear indentation on the soft brushed fabric blanket that served as Mireya's bedspread. It was rectangular and looked suspiciously suitcase-shaped to her. Opening Mireya's closet door revealed empty coat hangers in the center section, the likely area where she would keep her favorite and most frequently worn garments. A quick check of the top drawer in her low dresser revealed only a few undergarments remained. Rather than going to the police, Mireya had run.

By the time Regan went through the check-in process at the Santa Cruz Police Department on Center Street and received her visitor's badge, Regan had added another possible explanation for Mireya's disappearance, one she liked even less than that Mireya had made a run-for-it. She climbed the stairs and walked down the hall to Dave's office at the back of the second floor quickly, but she was still late.

"Half-an-hour?" he tapped the face of his watch. "Time must be different for you than it is for me."

"I'm sorry. I stopped by Mireya's house on the way. It's good I did, too, because I made a significant discovery. She's gone."

Dave sat bolt-upright in his seat. "What do you mean gone? I'm pretty sure she was told to stay close to home."

"Gone as in, from what I observed, she took a suitcase with her."

Dave wasn't one to swear, but he did.

"I just don't know whether she left on her own or was taken. Either way I have an idea where she may be going. I also know who she gave her money to."

"You know who she hired to kill her mother?" Dave's voice was unusually high as he questioned her.

"I know who she gave the money to, but according to her, she didn't hire him to do anything to her mom, although he may have."

"We gotta' get her back. I can listen with one ear while I fill out an APB. Start talkin'."

"You might want to tell the police to pay special attention to Canadian entry points. My guess is she's on her way there. She paid the money to her son's father, Hunter — I don't know his last name. Another thing I don't know, wouldn't even hazard a guess about, is whether she's running with him or to him, going there to make sure when the authorities talk to him his story matches hers, or whether he's kidnapped her."

Dave stopped typing and raised his eyes from his computer. "Wow." He quickly returned his attention to his computer. "Why Canada?" Dave asked, as his fingers began clicking away on his keyboard once more.

"Mireya said Hunter's family lives in Vancouver. She also said he told her he wanted to buy a house about an hour inland from there and that he had a good job, so he must be based within an hour radius of Vancouver. And since Vancouver sits on the coast, the search should be narrowed."

"That's a reasonable assumption," Dave nodded, as he finished typing. "Knowing you and the way your mind works,

I'm gonna' bet you have an opinion about whether your little maybe-hitman-hiring gal pal is running or being dragged," he challenged.

Regan shook her head. "That's a bad bet; I don't know what to think. Mireya said Martha had been paying Hunter to stay out of her and Jackson's lives, something she didn't know until he told her right before Martha was murdered, so add making Jackson's father disappear as another potential reason for Mireya to hate her mother. She said Hunter told her the payments were ending because Martha was out of money, so put a check in the box that said he had motive to harm Martha for free. Mireya said he was threatening a custody fight for her son so she offered him money to forget it. She said he was offended and spoke disparagingly about her and her mother, but then took her money. So what does all that mean? And then she said he told her he would settle up with both of them. Mireya didn't know if that was a threat, so I certainly don't know, either.

"When I saw Mireya yesterday afternoon, I offered to go with her to the police station. She said I didn't need to, that she'd do it on her own. I'm kicking myself for not insisting I at least bring her to see you myself."

Dave rolled his head in a circle like he was trying to get out a kink in his neck. "Don't be so hard on yourself, Regan. She's good, maybe the best liar we've had through here in a while."

"Unless she's not lying about anything and is in trouble."

Dave bobbed his head up and down slowly. "Yeah."

With the whole Mireya escapade, Regan had pushed Roya Matthew's bad behavior to a deep forgotten spot in her mind, but once she accepted that there was nothing she could do about Mireya's disappearance, it resurfaced.

Roya's shenanigans picked an inopportune time to pester her, too. Tom had suggested dinner at Avanti, which should have meant a quiet, even romantic, time at one of Santa Cruz's finer restaurants. But rather than being able to enjoy a lovely meal with her husband, Regan found herself in full-on conspiracy mode.

She talked non-stop about her tour of the empty lots in the proposed Rancho Grande Village and the ongoing legal maneuvers various citizen's groups had used to stop its development, using her salad fork to punctuate her statements.

"If that wasn't enough," Regan's words tumbled out with increasing energy and speed, "even if the project had been approved, Roya Matthews got Martha to offer an insanely large amount of money for an undeveloped lot."

Tom shrugged. "Even if Roya Matthews did get Martha Varner into an investment that may have been disadvantageous," he said calmly, "you know how hard it is to prove intent, which you'd need to do if she was going to be charged with an ethics violation."

"But, but," Regan sputtered, "she was double ending the transaction; it makes what she did so obviously unethical."

"Maybe she genuinely thought the litigation had ended and everything was settled," Tom proposed, "and that the property would skyrocket in value."

"That's exactly why I've got to get my hands on a copy of Martha's purchase contract," Regan said, her voice full of frustration. "The dates on it will be incredibly revealing. I want to know if the offer was made after it looked like the Village was approved or after it was clear new litigation had started, meaning it absolutely wasn't going forward in the foreseeable future."

"Promise me you won't stab me with your fork," Tom teased, "but for the sake of argument, suppose the dates show what you think they will. What happens next? The principle in the transaction who stood to be harmed is dead."

"Her daughter isn't," Regan said, as she put her fork down and picked up her water glass and took a sip. "What Roya Matthews did affects Mireya's living arrangements and her inheritance. She'd have a case against Roya Matthews, wouldn't she?"

"Litigation is always unpredictable, but she might…unless she becomes a convicted murderess. That could affect what a jury might do for her in a negative way."

"I think a case could be made that the next generation, which means darling toddler Jackson with his big brown eyes and sweet shy grin, was affected, too."

"You've missed your calling. You should be a trial lawyer, or at least write closing arguments for lawyers," Tom laughed.

"I've got to see the contract," Regan said emphatically. "Can you work any magic with her broker to get a copy?"

"If the tables were turned and Roya Matthew's broker wanted me to give her a copy of a contract you were involved in writing that was none of her business, what do you think I'd say?"

"But you'd know I would never do anything unethical, so it's not the same at all."

"Perhaps her broker thinks she'd never do anything unethical," he suggested with a tilt of his head.

Regan sighed, "So you think it's impossible to get a copy of the contract?"

"I didn't say that. I just think we need to approach her broker through a back door."

"What do you mean?" Regan asked.

"If Roya Matthews' broker got a request for information because of a murder investigation, well, if I got such an official request, I'd cooperate. I bet her broker would, too."

Regan beamed at her husband. "Have I mentioned lately how brilliant I think you are?"

"Not lately."

"Then let me bring us up to date. I think you're brilliant. I'll call Dave tomorrow morning and suggest the police ask for a copy of Martha's contract. I can tell him it might add weight to their theory that Mireya had motive to kill her mother.

"I can let him know Mireya said Roya Matthews told her Martha changed her trust because of the offer, too. From what Mireya said, it sounds like she didn't know about the change before her mother was killed, but that's another reason to see the contract. Dates on it can be matched against when Martha changed her trust, and that information could be used to suggest when Mireya might have known about the changes independent of when she said she did."

"Indeed. But I think I should be the one to call Dave," Tom suggested. "Trust me, I'll do a brilliant job of laying out everything you suggested. I'll even offer that we'd be more than willing to assess the contract, just to help out."

"Brilliant and devious, too. Oh, how I love you," Regan giggled.

"Thought you'd like an update," Dave said as he slapped a folder on Regan's desk. "I know Tom offered to help with this — he thought he was real subtle in the way he asked for it, but he's got a lot to learn about trying to manipulate a cop like me without me knowing it — and I know you're really the one who wants to see this. I made a copy for you so you can study it for as long as you like and I know I can count on you and Tom not to broadcast that fact."

"Thank you, Dave." Regan maintained some casual detachment and just lightly patted the contract folder as she spoke, but her fingers practically burned with excitement as she touched it. "You mentioned an update. Is there more you were going to tell me?"

"I know how bad you felt about letting your little gal-pal slip out of town so maybe you'll feel better when I tell you that you were right about her making a run to Canada and also to let you know that she's running, not being forced to go. She made it across the border before we could stop her, but the Canadian force is hot on her and that Hunter Gregson guy's trail and will have them in custody soon, so thanks for the tip about where to look for them."

"Gregson? How did the police discover what Hunter's last name is?"

Dave let out a little harrumph noise. "It took me about twenty seconds. After you left my office all distraught with guilt and worry, I coolly got on my computer, logged into county birth records, and found Mireya Varner's baby's birth certificate. She listed Hunter Gregson of Vancouver, Canada as her baby's daddy.

"After that, all I had to do was make a few calls to the Gregson listings in Vancouver until I connected with the widow Gregson who had a son named Hunter. She's a nice lady; we had a good little chat. She said she hadn't seen her son in a couple of weeks, but that he had stopped by after his trip to California. She gave me his phone number and told me he worked in Maple Ridge, which is about an hour's drive from her house. You said Hunter told Mireya Varner he was lookin' for places to buy about an hour outside of Vancouver, so everything got real easy."

"With that much to go on, why haven't the Canadian police picked up Mireya and Hunter yet?" Regan asked quizzically.

Dave bobbed his head left to right. "I wonder that, too. Canadian Mounties and all that lore aside, they seem to be struggling. The interesting thing is I asked Mrs. Gregson if she'd give me a call if she heard from her son. I got a call from her the next day saying Mireya came by that morning and dropped off her son. Gammy — that's what she's calling herself — is delighted to have the little guy stay with her for some indeterminate amount of time while Jackson's ma and pa attend to some business.

"So that's the whole update. See how being a good girl works? You got everything you wanted to know. Because you've been so helpful recently, I'll let you fill Tom in on the details." Dave smiled and waved goodbye as he headed out her office door.

Regan had the contract folder open before Dave had taken two steps down the hall. She pulled out her notes about Rancho Grande Village and put them next to the contract so comparison would be easy. The first thing she noted was what she expected to see: Martha had entered into a purchase contract after the news of another legal challenge had been filed which threatened to delay the development for — if the County Recorder's Office employee was right — possibly another decade.

As the listing agent for the development, Roya Matthews would have to be fully aware of the challenge. As the agent for Martha Varner, she would have to disclose that setback to her client. Failure to do so could put her license at risk and leave her and her broker open to suit. Regan quickly flipped the contract pages over to the end and there it was: a disclosure of the legal challenge and litigation signed and dated by Martha Varner. At the top of the document there was even a line which indicated Martha had read and understood the statement before she made her offer, which was initialed by her.

Roya Matthews had made sure she was covered, but why had Martha, an intelligent, capable woman, agreed to such a thing? What had Roya said to her? How had Roya persuaded her client to make an offer in spite of an obviously impossible situation? Roya must have told Martha something not in the clearly written document that had influenced her, but without Martha's testimony as to their conversation, all that remained was Roya's perfectly crafted CYA — cover your ass — document which would stand up and protect her in any courtroom or mediation.

There was a second addendum to the contract. It was a contingency creating statement:

Completed blueprints for three possible homes to be built within Rancho Grande Village will be provided by Mathius Royce Hugel, NAAB certified.

1. *A triplex, or if construction of a triplex is not allowed in Rancho Grande Village,*

2. *A duplex of unequal proportions, or if construction in Rancho Grande Village is limited to single family units,*

3. *A single-family home designed to provide excellent separation for three family units living within the same structure.*

All three blueprint options shall be approved by buyer, Martha Varner before close of escrow.

So Martha had intended to provide a home for Mireya and Jackson in Carmel. Her first choice appeared to be a triplex. Who else did Martha plan to have live in close proximity, Regan wondered? Judi? Probably not in one of the triplexes, since Martha had only suggested Judi might join her in Carmel well after the contract was signed. Martha's newly discovered son? That was an interesting thought.

Regan had worked with Martha in the past and had learned she was one of those clients who chatted. Before they became friends, when Martha was still only her client, Martha had been open and excited to share personal information with her, and if Martha had done that with her during their professional relationship, Regan was sure Martha had burbled about her plans with Roya Matthews. Roya must have known Martha had discovered her abandoned son. With luck, Martha might have mentioned his name to Roya or at least given her some information about him, possibly enough that Regan could figure out who he was and connect him with his half-sister, Mireya.

Regan flipped the contract back to the signature page. The contract was signed by Roya Matthews, who had power of attorney for Mathius Royce Hugel. It was not unexpected that Roya would be given that authority — Mireya told her she was to send her rent check made out to Roya Matthews — but her mind swirled with her discovery of who the seller was and what that meant. What were the chances the property owner just happened to be an architect ready to design properties for Martha? But since he was, he must be competent enough to sign a contract. So why would he turn over power of attorney to Roya Matthews? Was he in hiding for some reason?

She also wondered which came first, the property or the architectural plans? And how did Roya, with her power of attorney for the seller/architect, fit into the order of things?

Tom walked past her office, clients in tow, waived an acknowledgement to her, and headed for his office. She was desperate to talk to him, but knew better than to interrupt him when he was conducting business. She returned to the contract.

All the usual boxes were checked and uninteresting and she skimmed quickly until she got to the financing section. Roya's language made it clear that, even if a copy of the contract had been available before escrow closed, Mireya had no wiggle room to escape the sale of her house and her mother's condo once her mother signed escrow instructions. The amount credited for both properties was fair — she couldn't fault Roya Matthews for selling out her client by undervaluing her property — and their titles were signed over to Mathius Royce Hugel as part of the payment due for the title to 60 Casitas Road, Carmel Valley, California.

She could complain about what Martha had agreed to pay for her purchase, however. Again, the number was expected after she read it while visiting the Monterey County Recorder's office, but $1,900,000 for so far useless land and architectural drawings? The purchase contract added insult injury, Regan noted, because, in addition to the properties, Martha Varner had to add two-hundred-fifteen-thousand-dollars to the pot at the close of escrow.

Roya had neatly hand-written an addendum stipulating Mireya Varner could rent her property for a period of six months after close of escrow for the same amount she currently paid her mother for her mortgage. Regan noted a nasty sounding sentence stating, "Failure to keep rental payments current shall vacate the rental agreement immediately." The statement was cold but correct; Roya's work was clear, concise, and appropriate.

Regan hoped Tom was finished with his clients. She walked up the hall to his office clutching the contract. Tom's two clients — older and well-dressed — were still there sitting with their backs to her in chairs that faced his desk. Regan stared through Tom's window like a starving Dickensian child surveying baked goods in a store window, willing them to finish-up and leave. She thought about pressing her fingertips and nose against his window dramatically, but decided against it.

At that moment, Tom and the man stood up and reached across Tom's desk to shake hands. The woman also rose and, after what seemed to Regan like an interminable exchange of pleasant words, Tom walked them to his office door and opened it. "I'll arrange for the painting and repairs we discussed and send photos to you when the work is completed. Have a safe flight home," Tom said.

Once the couple shook Tom's hand one more time, said goodbye, and headed down the hall to the back entrance and parking, Tom grabbed his wife's arm and pulled her into his office. "Your impatience is showing," he chided. "What's on your mind that's so urgent?"

"Take a look at this. It's Martha Varner's purchase contract. The date on it proves it was drawn up after development of Rancho Grande Village went back into litigation. Roya Matthews may have disclosed that information to Martha, but getting her to buy this property, I think she was still playing fast and loose ethically."

"I thought you were searching for evidence in the contract that might help prove Mireya Varner's innocence."

"I was," Regan equivocated, "but Roya Matthews…"

"You don't like her very much, do you?" Tom interrupted.

"No, I don't. I think she took advantage of Martha to make a sale."

Tom flipped through the contract pages. "Interesting," he said when he read the addendums. "You understand, this isn't any of your business, though, don't you?"

Regan evaded his question with eager questions of her own. "Should Mireya speak with an attorney? Do you think she may have some legal recourse to reverse the sale or sue Roya Matthews?"

"Honestly?" Tom dropped the contract on his desk, "What Roya Matthews did doesn't look good — if one of our agents did this, I'd be asking them to find another brokerage — but it doesn't appear to be unlawful, either. She's disclosed that the property had reentered litigation and made it clear she was representing both sides of the transaction. Martha signed off on both things. Short of Martha's testimony that Roya Matthews mislead her when she explained what the documents meant, there's no perusable misconduct here. I think Mireya would be wasting her time and money with an attorney."

"But with Roya having the listing and power of attorney for the seller and representing Martha, doesn't that add up to something unethical?" Regan asked, frustration echoing in her voice.

Tom shook his head. "Now, if Roya owned the property and was also representing both sides of the sale, she'd be doing something unethical, even illegal, but her just having power of attorney for the seller doesn't rise to the same level of engagement. Sorry, Sweetheart. Technically Roya

Matthews didn't do anything wrong. Please don't take this to heart so much that you turn into a moral scold."

Regan spent the rest of her workday involved with clients. An offer arrived on one of her listings which meant a meeting with her sellers, and she had a signoff with a delightful couple buying their first home, one of her favorite things to do, so she was able to put the question of Mireya's runaway and Martha's contract out of her mind during the day.

Both issues resurfaced as she lay in bed and kept her from restful sleep. She decided a cup of tea was in order.

As Regan stood by the stove in her pajamas, watching steam begin to escape from the kettle and waiting for the perfect moment when the water was hot enough to brew tea but still hadn't sounded its shrill Tom-waking whistle, she heard the wrought iron gate to the courtyard creak faintly. The sound was unmistakable: someone had opened it. Someone was in the courtyard.

Regan turned off the kettle and quickly switched on the courtyard lights. A suddenly illuminated Mireya stood with her raised hand made into a fist ready to knock on the sliding glass door to the kitchen. A tall young man stood behind her, his hands jammed into his jacket pockets. Regan moved to the door and slid it open.

"Mireya!" Regan was so startled that she didn't try to keep her voice low. "What are you...come in."

Tom, awakened by the commotion, rushed into the kitchen still fuzzy from sleep. "What's going on?" he quizzed.

"I'm sorry," Mireya stumbled through a rambling apology. "We found your address. I know it's late, I'm sorry if I scared you. I promised you I'd go to the police, but I decided not to. I thought I should explain why I ran away. This is Hunter. He's Jackson's father. I went to Canada to find him. I left Jackson with Hunter's mom. She's a nice woman. I thought Jackson should meet his other grandma, especially now that my mom…" she halted her tumble of words by biting her lip.

Regan put her arm around Mireya and hugged her. "The police are actively looking for you. You need to turn yourself in before the police find you. Hunter, they want to talk to you, too. Let me call my friend in the police department and ask him how to get you into their hands voluntarily and without a lot of fuss, okay?"

Mireya nodded.

"Yes, ma'am," Hunter added.

"I bet it's been a long night for you two and it's probably going to be a lot longer. I'll get us all some coffee," Tom offered, "while Regan makes her call.

Regan went to her office, closed the door, and peered at her clock. It read 12:53. She had no idea which of her friends would answer, but she knew she'd wake both of them. She took a deep breath, already mentally apologizing to both of them, and dialed Dave and Sandy's home number.

Dave answered with a grumpy, "You know what time it is? Are you guys okay?"

"Yes, Dave, Tom and I are fine. I'm so sorry to call you at this hour."

"Then explain: why me, why now, Regan?"

She could tell by the drop in his voice's volume that he had turned his head away away from the phone. She heard him reassuring Sandy, "Everyone's fine. It's just Regan calling with some no-doubt fascinating story to tell me that couldn't wait until morning. Go back to sleep, honey."

It took a minute before he spoke again, but when he did, he was clearly holding the phone to his mouth once more. "You callin' at this hour and waking us up; there better be blood involved," he said curtly.

"No blood, Dave. Tom's making coffee for Mireya Varner and her son's father, Hunter."

"What!"

"They're in our kitchen. They want to turn themselves in. I didn't think they should be driving around town going to the police station. I told them you'd know how to arrange for a safe surrender. Promise no guns, Dave," Regan pleaded.

She heard something unintelligible that might have been swearing or merely mystification coming from Dave.

"I'll get a couple of duty officers to come to your house. No guns, Regan. But there will be handcuffs. Prepare your little gal pal and her baby daddy for that."

"Thank you," Regan said weakly.

"Sure. Anytime. Anytime between the hours of 7:00 am and 10:00pm, that is."

🏠🏠🏠🏠🏠🏠🏠🏠🏠🏠🏠

Regan took Dave chocolate chip cookies baked from the dough she always had at the ready in her freezer for baking at open houses, cookie props as it were, to entice buyers by making a house seem homey. She also brought good coffee from Kelley's to accompany them so, should he decide to dunk them in his coffee — something she'd seen him do many times and which she found abhorrent — their flavor wouldn't be compromised by police station brown water trying to pass for coffee. Her final offering to him was the copy of the contract he had given Tom by way of her so it could ostensibly be checked for incriminating evidence against Mireya Varner.

"I'm sorry for last night's late call, but at least I got you Mireya and Hunter."

"Having prime suspects Uno and Dos in custody hardly makes up for making Sandy groggy on her drive to work over Highway 17," he complained.

"No, I guess not, but I hope the cookies will at least help you feel better," she smiled empathetically.

He dumped the contract copy into his waste basket. "Don't need this," and peeled the cup-topper off his coffee, "do need this." He selected a cookie from the bag and dunked. "FYI, chocolate never hurts and that's not limited to women."

Regan jumped right to the point of her visit. "Do you still think Mireya's guilty?"

Dave said nothing until he finished swallowing another dunked cookie. "Their stories matched, I'll give you that, but, then, they've had days together and plenty of time to practice what they were going to say."

"I thought the police had interrogators who were trained in the fine art of tripping up suspects who fabricated their stories."

"We do. And your little gal-pal and her boyfriend got split up right away and questioned all night so they were tired and at a disadvantage. Bottom line is they told the same story and consistently, but with enough variation in wording that our guys think they may be telling the truth."

"Was Hunter willing to give you a DNA sample?"

"Willing and so eager it was almost embarrassing. We should have our answer if he's a match by tomorrow morning."

"If he's not the killer, that means both he and Mireya are innocent."

"Boing, boing, boing. There you go jumpin' to conclusions faster than the winner at the Calaveras County frog jumping contest."

"I'm not jumping to anything," Regan protested. "If Hunter didn't kill Martha and Judi, Mireya couldn't have hired him, so she's innocent of involvement in their murder, too."

"She could have still hired some other guy."

"With what? She drained her bank account and gave the money to Hunter. Even you have to agree with that. So unless hit-men take credit cards, no money, no hire." Regan was so proud of her reasoning that she dunked a cookie in her coffee without realizing it.

"Your little Mireya is an attractive woman. There are other ways to pay for services rendered," Dave fired back.

"You're stretching and you know it."

Dave shrugged. "Credit it to my lack of sleep last night." He sighed loudly. "Yeah, it looks like Mireya and her guy are probably dead ends," he confessed. "They have been told not to leave town, though, just in case something turns up.

"In the meantime, we're gonna' have to start over, rethink everything, and we will. But at the moment, we don't have any great ideas…and if you ever tell anyone what I just said, I'll deny it until I can swear I never said any such thing on the stack of cold bibles we collected from hell after it froze over. Am I clear enough for you?"

11

Regan sat in Roya Matthews office and smiled sweetly. "Would you like to give Mireya Varner a copy of her mother's contract or should she get one from her mother's attorney?"

"Is that the same attorney who will be defending her on murder charges?" Roya, in a summer-weight golden outfit, her metal-of-the-day color choice, grinned back, her big smile as artificial as Regan's was.

"You keep surprisingly good tabs on my client, Roya. Why does Mireya Varner interest you so?"

"Your client? When did she become your client?"

"Mireya, who has not been charged with anything, especially not murder, by the way, has asked me to represent her in trying to decide whether she should be consulting an attorney — a real estate attorney, not her mother's estate attorney — about the purchase contract you drew up and Martha signed."

"On what basis? I explained all aspects of what Martha signed clearly, she agreed to go forward, and she signed off on my explanations. If written documents are called into question, what I told Martha becomes a she said/she said argument, and with only one half of the parties to the contract present to testify, who do you think will be believed?"

Roya batted her long eyelashes rapidly as she explained her position and color rose in her cheeks. It might have been that Roya was flustered under her composed exterior, Regan thought, or it might be that she was simply furious at being challenged. If she had to guess, Regan would have gone with the latter explanation.

Regan, still smiling, pressed on. "Of course. I'm certain you did a perfect job of documenting everything. But I stopped by the Monterey County Records Department in Salinas after our last little visit, so I know what Martha bought and how much she paid for it. And it's just that, well," Regan threw out a casual little chuckle, "it does seem odd that a woman of Martha's age would buy a property for as much money as she spent without the expectation that it was buildable in the immediate future."

"There had been litigation to stop development of the property, but that had been settled by the courts when Martha made her purchase."

"Umm," Regan, pressed her lips together and shook her head, "are you sure? I agree that the courts had given permission for development of Rancho Grande Village, but when did Martha sign her purchase contract? I wonder because a new suit to halt development was filed within days of the old litigation being settled. I believe a story about the new litigation was reported in Carmel's paper, *The Carmel Pine Cone*, and as the listing agent, you must have been aware of that. Surely you informed Martha of that new litigation," Regan asked with saccharin tones, "didn't you?"

"Of course I did. But the new suit was merely a nuisance suit. Martha recognized that and thought the new litigation would be resolved quickly."

"But even if Martha believed her parcel would be buildable soon, what about the price she agreed to pay for it? Wasn't that kind of high?" Regan didn't wait for an answer. "You know how it looks when an agent double-ends a transaction that seems to favor one side over the other. Ethical questions can be so messy, can't they?"

"You wouldn't know it and neither would Ms. Varner, because you haven't seen the contract yet, but the purchase included sets of architectural designs for three separately configured dwellings drawn up by a prominent architect. Each of those designs is quite valuable and Martha had the right to approve of all three before her contract conditions were removed. If you deduct the cost of designing three structures and creating blueprints for them, let's just say with that valuable consideration, the price Martha offered was fair, perfectly fair."

The high color had slipped away from Roya's cheeks as she continued. Regan interpreted that as a signal that Roya felt she was once again in control of the conversation.

Regan saw no need to tell her that she was indeed aware of the plans. "A prominent architect? Knowing Martha, I bet she was excited about that. Would I recognize the architect's name?"

"I'm not sure. He's from the East Coast, from Connecticut, and is a member the NAAB."

"The NAAB?"

"The National Architectural Accrediting Board. It's a highly regarded group."

"And how was Martha fortunate enough to have him involved in her purchase contract?" Regan knew the answer to her question, but she wanted to hear Roya's explanation.

"Well," Roya twittered with amusement, "it's an interesting coincidence, but he happens to be the former owner of Martha's property."

Regan pounced. "You mean the architect and seller are the same person?"

"Yes."

"So he lives here now? When did he move here from, Connecticut, did you say?"

Color once again began to creep under Roya's makeup to tinge her cheeks. "He doesn't live here, actually."

Regan made a knowing head nod. "Oh, Mireya said you have power of attorney for the seller and that she is to make her rent checks out to you. That explains why. Having power of attorney for him makes everything so much easier, doesn't it? With him on the other side of the country, you can sign on his behalf after a quick phone conversation. No taxing mailing or even emailing, faxing, or copious texting and documents to be printed out."

"Yes. Exactly."

Regan paused as if a question had just occurred to her. "When, or perhaps the right word is how, did this renowned architect who doesn't live locally come to own a parcel of land in Rancho Grande Village?"

The tip of Roya's tongue showed in the corner of her mouth but disappeared before it traversed more than half-way across her lips. "He travels sometimes. He likes to find places where he, where his talents, might be appreciated. Occasionally he buys a property with the idea of developing it. He says nothing works better to win business than to have a home representing his work that potential clients can see up close. It's kind of like having a living portfolio available for prospective clients. He purchased a couple of lots in the Rancho Grande Village development with the intent of developing them for show. Unfortunately, he was unable to complete his plans because of the litigation, but like Martha, he expects the issue to be resolved soon.

"Since escrow has closed and you are representing Mireya Varner, let me get a copy of the contract complete with the full blueprints for you. Just give me a quick little moment to run it by my broker to be absolutely sure I'm not doing anything I shouldn't."

Roya rose and, looking like a golden award stature, strode elegantly from her office, leaving Regan sitting alone facing Roya's empty desk. She was back quicker than Regan expected — clearly she wasn't leaving Regan to solitarily fidget as a final power play — and handed her a sizable packet.

"Are you sure you wouldn't like to give this to Mireya yourself?" Regan asked. "You've never met her."

"No need. The contract stipulates that I'll be the listing agent in the sale of her house in no more than six-months-time; I'll have a chance to meet her then."

Regan was aware of the stipulation, but pretended not to be, using her pretend surprise as a cover for asking a question that had been bothering her since she was first aware of the agreement.

"Oh? What a surprise. I would have assumed Martha would have designated me as the listing agent since, as a local agent, I would know property values well. And of course, we had done transactions before and become friends, too."

Roya leaned back in her chair with her elbows on the chair arms, pressed her palms together, and touched her extended fingers to her chin. "What can I say, Regan," she oozed out her words slowly. "Evidently Martha liked me better than she liked you."

🏠🏠🏠🏠🏠🏠🏠🏠🏠🏠🏠

"Mireya," Regan said over the phone, "I have a copy of the contract your mother signed. Could I come by and bring it to you?"

"I guess," Mireya hesitated, "although I don't know what difference it makes, seeing the contract now."

"I'd like to talk to you about it, and get myself off the hook, too."

"What do you mean?"

"I may have misrepresented the facts slightly to get it. I told your mother's Carmel real estate agent that I was representing you and would give you the contract. Make an honest woman of me, please."

"You're who I turned to when this whole mess started, so of course, you're representing me. Close the loop," Mireya sounded resigned. "Bring me the contract. Besides, I could use a good shoulder to cry on, well not cry on, complain to is more like it. You can come by any time. It seems I've been let go from my job — it was decided having an accused murderess teaching first grade was not in the best interest of the children — so I'm sitting here missing Jackson with nothing much to do anyway."

Regan's last client meeting ended at 2:45. She was sitting at Mireya's kitchen table a little after 3:00. Mireya poured them coffee in oversized mugs which she filled to the very brim, barely leaving room for the cream Regan would need to make drinking coffee tolerable.

Regan began by spreading the blueprints out on the table until they were flat. "Have a look, Mireya. These are part of the contract your mother signed for the Rancho Grande Village property. She was planning to take care of you and Jackson, Mireya, I want you to know that. She was going to build a multi-generational dwelling. Since she didn't yet know what the development's restrictions would be, she had three contingencies for living designed. The first..."

"It would have been nice if she asked me how I felt about moving to Carmel before she arranged my life, don't you think?" Mireya's tone of voice fell somewhere between wistful and angry.

"I think she was planning to tell you about it at the lunch she scheduled with you. The plans demonstrate she intended for three families to live together."

"Three?"

"Yes. She had designs for three separate self-sufficient spaces in one house as her worst possible case, but her first choice was to build a triplex."

"A triplex? Do you think she was planning to have Judi live with us?"

"It's possible, but Judi told me your mom suggested she make a move to Carmel after the contract was written, so I don't think Judi was who she had in mind."

"Who then?" Mireya asked. As soon as her question left her lips, her expression began to change. The answer began occurring to her even before Regan spoke.

"I think what Judi told me about your mother finding your half-brother is true and that Martha planned to reunite all of you in a sort of family compound in Carmel.

"Can't you imagine how your mother must have felt? Suppose you lost Jackson and thought you would never see him again, married and had another child, and then rediscovered him. Of course, your mom shouldn't have made decisions affecting you without first talking to you about them, but can't you understand her excitement at the thought of having her whole family together once more. Her elation could have clouded her judgement."

"So you think it's true then, that I do have a half-brother. It was okay when he was a possibility, but now that he's real, I don't know how to process that," Mireya said in a voice barely above a whisper. "And if he's real, why hasn't he contacted me?"

"I think the question is does he know about you or was your mother planning to tell him about you at that lunch in

Carmel? She may have been planning to introduce you to one another that day. If he doesn't know about you, that may explain why you haven't heard from him. But if you want to try and find him, I have an idea about how to reach out to him."

Mireya looked up at Regan with puppy-dog eyes. "How?"

"Since he seems to have walked in the Monterey SPCA fundraiser, let's assume he lives in the Carmel area. If he does, he'll be a reader of *The Carmel Pine Cone*. Carmel is unlike most places, it's small and tightly knit. People who live there still have to go to the post office to pick up their mail. Everyone reads that newspaper for their fix of local gossip. If we run an ad in it asking for the son of the late Martha Varner to contact us, he should see it. Hopefully he'll act on the request. We might even broaden the ad so other people might respond with his name. We could say he may own a Chevalier King Charles Spaniel, possibly named Queeny. That should make who he is pretty clear to a number of *Pine Cone* readers. I bet we'll get a good lead from one of them, if not from your brother himself."

"Let's do it," Mireya said excitedly.

Regan smiled, "Try to keep your hopes in check, will you, Mireya, in case this doesn't work."

"I want it to so badly." Mireya answered wistfully.

"There is another thing I wanted to talk to you about. I did look at the contract and there is a possibility that you have some legal recourse against Roya Matthews. It's a long shot, but something you may want to persue."

"Let's not do that. I don't want any more interaction with courts and the authorities than I've already had. I'm burned out, Regan, and nothing seems to be ending. All I want to do is go back to Canada with Hunter, hug Jackson, and try to get on with my life. Hunter has asked me to marry him and I'm planning to say yes, if this investigation ever ends and I'm once again a truly free woman."

"You plan to marry Hunter? You said you wouldn't settle for a husband, didn't you?"

"I'm not settling." Mireya smiled shyly and seemed to blush slightly. "I was madly in love with Hunter when Jackson was conceived, but his history scared me. And then I thought he had abandoned us, when he hadn't. Now he's demonstrated what he did as a teenager isn't what he'll do as an adult. He really did save every penny my mother sent to bribe him and worked hard to save his own money, too, all so he could buy a house for us to live in as a family. I'm not settling, Regan. I love him and now think he's ready to be a good husband and father.

"The only problem is the police have told me I can't leave until they finish their investigation."

"I thought they cleared Hunter."

"They did, but that doesn't mean they've given up on me. They keep trying to find a man I got to do my bidding. They dragged in a guy who does some gardening work for me a couple of times a year, oh, and the latest is my aerobics instructor.

"He's a type one diabetic like I am. Exercise is important for both of us to maintain our health. Peter is able to earn a living doing something he needs to do every day and I go to his classes regularly, that's our big connection. But when the police found out he has a supply of insulin..." she rolled her eyes. "It's embarrassing, Regan. I had dinner with him a couple of times, innocent dinners because we're friends with the same disease, who like to talk occasionally, no invites to come in for coffee or anything else after. To hear the police tell it, though, you'd think I've been sleeping with every guy I come in contact with, trying to seduce someone into killing Mom and Judi."

"I'm so sorry you're having to go through this," Regan sympathized. "They'll figure out who the killer is, hopefully soon. While you wait, let's see if we can find you some family close by."

Regan, who wrote house ads several times a week, volunteered to write *The Carmel Pine Cone* ad. She spent much more time working on it than she expected, agonizing over every word and every comma. When she thought it read right, she slipped into Tom's office to ask his opinion.

"Can I read this to you?" she asked.

"Sure, what is it?"

"An ad aimed at Mireya's half-brother or anyone who may have information about him. I'm thinking it should read:

*Seeking contact with or information about deceased Santa Cruz resident Martha Varner's son. His sister and toddler nephew want him to be part of their family. The only information they have about him is that he lives in or near Carmel and has a Chevalier King Charles Spaniel which may be named Queeny. If you know him, please bring this ad to his attention, or if you have any suggestions about how to find him, please call...*and then I put in my cell phone number so Amanda wouldn't have to field responses.

"I think that's a good ad."

"It doesn't sound too assertive?"

"Not at all. The line about the little nephew and wanting to find him so he can be part of their family is a nice, compelling touch."

Regan emailed the ad to *The Carmel Pine Cone* and scheduled it to run for the next four editions in various parts of the newspaper. Since the paper came out on Fridays, was only published weekly, and since she placed the ad on Tuesday with the deadline for the main section due the Friday before ads ran, she had more than a week to wait before she could expect a flood of callers from Carmel.

Her lead time did mean she could request placement on the Sandy Claws column page, near the regularly scheduled Animal Friends Rescue Project ad, which ran weekly and featured pictures of adorable kittens and puppies dressed up for themed events. She expected the Queeny connection might play well there and jog the memories of Carmel's animal lovers. She also requested a random main section placement and placement again near the Sandy Claws column for the second week, one in the obituaries section on week three, and the final one in the paper's real estate section, because it was made up about two-fifths of the paper.

🏠🏠🏠🏠🏠🏠🏠🏠🏠🏠🏠

When Regan called Mireya three days after the first ad ran with nothing more to say than that no one had called her, she expected Mireya to sound dejected. Instead, she got a jubilant woman on the other end of her phone.

"It doesn't matter, Regan. The police have agreed to let me leave. I'm flying to Vancouver tomorrow afternoon. All I have to do is give them a viable phone number and address where I can be reached and leave them a DNA sample before I go. I'm so excited," she gushed.

"That's great news, Mireya. Does that mean they cleared you?"

Mireya laughed harshly. "No. It means Canada has a strong extradition agreement with the U.S. They made it clear they want my DNA in case anything comes up — I don't know, maybe an insulin syringe that rolled under a rug at a crime scene that everyone missed with my DNA on it — but I can leave. I can see Jackson again, and Hunter — he went back home last week — and have an almost normal life again, maybe even begin planning a wedding.

"Regan, I appreciate all your efforts, but I'm happy for the first time since all this started, so the fact that my brother hasn't turned up doesn't seem very important to me right now."

"I understand. Since I've scheduled the ads, though, I think I'll let them run. An abundance of family wouldn't be a bad thing, would it?"

"Not at all. I'd love to have him at my wedding. And you and Tom, too. I guess Hunter and I should do something small and simple, but I've never been a bride before and I want a big production. It will take some time to plan, so I'll give you plenty of warning when it's to be."

"We'll be there, Mireya."

It was more than a week before Regan saw Dave again, since she didn't have a crisis that made her finagle a pass to his office in the Santa Cruz Police Department building, and she didn't attempt to bribe him for information with a hand-delivered bag of scones or sweets. She ran into him in an unexpected place: waiting in line to pay for a can of spray paint at San Lorenzo Lumber on River Street.

"You plannin' on tagging something, Regan?" his familiar voice called out from three people behind her. "You can get arrested for that, ya know."

"It's white paint, Dave, too boring for doing any graffiti art."

The busy contractors waiting in line meant she couldn't give him cuts, so she let the next three customers move ahead of her and joined him further back in line. "I've been meaning to call you."

"Yeah, I've been expecting you to, and no, we haven't figured out who killed your pals."

"I know you haven't; you would have called me to crow with that kind of news. Does your long silence mean the investigation is stalled?"

He shrugged, "You could say that. We kicked your little gal pal loose, or at least let her leave town with a long bungee cord attached to her, but you probably already knew that."

"I did. She invited Tom and me to the wedding she and Hunter are planning in Canada. Do you think she's going to be free to turn up at it in a few months?"

"Some of the guys still like her for offing her mom, but me, I say, yeah. We got nothing that ties her to the crime. Problem is we got nothing that ties anybody to the crime and time's passing. Once you get a coupla' months distant from the last killing without any idea who did it, things tend to bog down."

"So you're giving up?" Regan's question made Dave an integral part of the investigation team, something he often did himself, but coming from her, his inclusion pushed one of his buttons.

"I don't make those sorts of decisions. If it was up to me, I'd still be keeping it a priority to find the killer. All I'm sayin is realistically, it's not looking good right now."

The two contractors in front of them had turned back to face them, intrigued by what was being said.

Dave flicked his hand at them, "The line's moving; you should be, too."

"I guess that means you wouldn't mind if I gave figuring out what happened a try?"

Dave rolled several parts of himself: his eyes, his head, and his shoulders. "Pros, cops who do every day haven't a clue, but you, a realator — he made sure to pronounce her profession in an incorrect and annoying manner — are gonna' solve the crime. Knock yourself out."

"Thanks for your blessing," Regan said as she was called forward to pay for her spray paint. "You go ahead," she said to Dave. "There's something I forgot to get."

Tom discovered Regan in her office placing a 3' x 3' foot piece of plywood she had covered with stick-on whiteboard on a tripod placed across from her desk to the right of her plaid Buchanan chairs.

"What's up, Sweetheart?"

"I'm going pro. I ran into Dave and he said the police have no leads in Martha and Judi's murders. He gave me permission to solve the crimes."

"Dave gave you permission?" Tom raised his eyebrows and grinned, "You don't say?"

"Well, maybe not exactly, but he didn't say not to."

"And the board on a tripod?"

"Professional police use boards like this to solve crimes. They usually add photos of everyone involved, but I didn't think it was necessary."

Tom's laughter was warm and filled with good humor.

"You're laughing at me!"

"Umm, perhaps, but let's just say I'm amused by you and let it go at that."

Regan did her best to scowl, but with Tom even that was hard for her. She opted instead to get out her whiteboard marker and begin writing. She wrote Dr. Goatt, Mireya, Jimmy, Hunter, exercise instructor, and Person Unknown across the top of the board and drew neat vertical lines to the bottom of the board to separate the names into columns.

Tom sat on her sofa, crossed his legs at the ankle and questioned her. "I thought the exercise instructor, Jimmy, and Hunter had been ruled out because their DNA didn't match the skin samples under Judi's fingernails and, since the method used to kill both women was unusual and the same, it was assumed that both had the same killer? Doesn't that mean you have to rule them out?"

Regan produced the specially manufactured eraser that came with the marker and erased three columns. On the left side of the board just below the remaining names, she wrote Murder Weapon: insulin and drew a horizontal line to the right side of the board. She put a check in the created box under Dr. Goatt and Mireya's names because they had access to the drug. She paused for a minute and put a check under Person Unknown, too.

Next, she wrote Opportunity/Trust below Murder Weapon and drew another horizontal line. Her checks were already becoming more complicated. Dave said Dr. Goatt had an alibi for the time of Judi's murder and it seemed unlikely that either woman would have invited him into their homes. Rather than a check, she put a question mark and decided his alibi needed closer scrutiny.

Mireya would have been welcomed into either woman's home, but she was in police custody at the time of Judi's murder. Regan left the space blank

Under Person Unknown, since she didn't know who that might be, she put a check in the box.

Finally, she wrote DNA: Male and drew a line. Checks went into Dr. Goatt's box and into Person Unknown's box.

"Why are you checking Dr. Goatt's box for DNA? Didn't the police collect a sample from him and rule him out?" Tom asked.

"As far as I know they never went that far. He had a weighty alibi so they stopped investigating him. I've never been convinced about him, though. I can imagine his witness covering for him and saying she was assisting him with his spaying and neutering the morning Judy was killed, either because she benefitted financially from the scam he was running or because of something personal."

"Personal? You think he has something, blackmail possibly, on her that he's using to get her to lie for him?"

Regan smiled sweetly. "No. I'm a hopeless romantic. I think she might be in love with him…"

"In love with him?" Tom protested loudly. "Have you seen the man?"

"You can't explain love only by considering how someone looks, especially when it comes to women. We are a forgiving sex. We love our men for many reasons and often how they look never enters into it."

"Are you saying you'd still love me if I had brown eyes?" Tom teased.

"I'd love you if you had one brown eye and one purple eye. Now if you weren't smart, I might have a problem. It's your brain I find sexy," she giggled, "well, and some other parts of you, too.

"Having this whiteboard in front of me and organized is heartening. I can see why police use these things. It's given me an idea where to start. And you know how important it is to me to have a plan."

🏠🏠🏠🏠🏠🏠🏠🏠🏠🏠🏠

"SPCA of Santa Cruz," a friendly voice pronounced over the background noise of dogs barking not too far from the phone. "We have no lions, tigers, or bears, but we do have adorable kittens and puppies, senior animals, bunnies, and all sorts or wonderful critters waiting to love you."

Regan hadn't been inside the SPCA since it moved to its new location on Chanticleer Avenue and so had not met any of the staff, but based on the phone answerer's greeting, she was sure the staff and volunteers were as dedicated to the animals housed there as they had ever been.

"And I want to love one of them back," she replied. "I understand you have a wonderful veterinarian who volunteers there sometimes. I'm interested in adopting a senior dog and I was hoping I could come by, and before I fell too far in love with my new potential companion, ask the vet a few questions about caring for an older dog."

"Yes. We do have a lovely doctor who volunteers here one morning a week and one afternoon. His name is Dr. Goatt, and I'm sure he'd be delighted to speak with you."

"When will he be in this week?"

"Tomorrow morning between 9:00 and noon and Friday afternoon between 1:00 and 3:00."

"Perfect," Regan said quickly and ended her call.

At 9:35 the following morning, Regan, wearing huge sunglasses, layers of colorful loose draped linen, and a flowing flowered scarf wrapped around her neck and trailing down to her waist, burst into Dr. Goatt's office, confident he wouldn't be in house.

"Insurance companies!" she proclaimed to the woman manning the reception desk.

The past-middle-aged woman behind the desk blinked rapidly and asked, "May I help you?" rather hesitantly. Regan had her target.

"Well, I certainly hope so! No one else seems to be able to. Have you dealt with pet insurance companies before?"

"I have; that's part of my job. What seems to be the problem?"

"I received a bill for my cat Harry's neutering from Dr. Goatt, but my carrier says they have no evidence Harry was ever neutered here or anywhere else, so they are refusing to pay for his surgery. I know the date, if not the precise hour Dr. Goatt neutered him. Can you straighten this out for me or do I have to throw a hissy fit with my insurance company?"

"I'm sure I can help you. It sounds like a simple paperwork glitch. You said your cat's name is Harry?"

"That's correct."

"And what is your name and when was the surgery performed?"

"My name is Thomasina Kiley. The surgery was on the morning of...just a minute," Regan fumbled in her purse and produced a slip of paper with the date of Judi's murder on it and thrust it toward the receptionist.

"Let's see. Harry Kiley, neuter." The receptionist frowned. "I'm sorry, ma'am. I do have a pet patient listing for Harry Kiley, owner, Tom Kiley, but I don't see his name on the list of surgeries performed that morning."

"What?! Look again. Kiley, K-i-l-e-y. And it's Thomasina, not Tom; perhaps that's the sloppy paperwork problem right there."

"No, ma'am. Harry Kiley was not neutered on that date." The receptionist was clearly becoming rattled by Regan's sharp demeanor, just what she was hoping would happen.

"Surgeries did take place that morning, didn't they?"

"Yes, ma'am, five of them."

"Look harder!" Regan was around the edge of the reception desk in a flash peering at the computer screen over the flustered woman's shoulder. "Let me look, too. Harry must be on the list," she insisted.

"No, ma'am. See? Abjian, Spoker. Smith, Harvey, and Nelson. No Kiley, I'm sorry."

"Well, I never!" Regan straightened up, threw her head back with affront, and flounced out of the office.

As soon as she got in her car, she quickly wrote Abjian, Spoker, Smith, Harvey, and Nelson on the waiting paper tablet she had there while the names and their spellings were fresh in her mind. Smith, Harvey, and Nelson were pretty common and ordinary names. They'd be hard to track, but Spoker, and especially Abjian? If she searched for those names, she was certain she could find at least one pet-owning client of Dr. Goatt's.

Regan was well aware of how many people no longer used land lines and therefore weren't listed in the meager tome that passed for today's phone book, but after her ease in overwhelming Dr. Goatt's receptionist and looking at his private computer listings, she was feeling lucky.

Abjian. There were two listings. She copied down the phone numbers and flipped to Spoker. She found a Spoken and a Spokley, but no Spoker. Abjian was going to have to do.

She was still high on adrenaline from her adventure and still in full story telling mode when she dialed the first number. If Dr. Goatt was genuine, all she'd do was enhance his reputation, she told herself, and if he wasn't, catching him in an alibi-breaking lie made what she was doing completely acceptable.

"Ms. Abjian?"

A female voice belonging to a heavy smoker greeted her query. "Yes."

"I'm doing a follow-up call from Dr. Goatt's office concerning your animal companion."

"Edie?"

A hit on the first call. Regan had to rein in her excitement. "Yes, about Edie. We were wondering how she's doing after her spay operation."

"Well, fine, I think. She was a little down after it just like Dr. Goatt said she would be, but she perked right up within a day or two and she's all healed up well now."

"That's good to hear."

"Yes, and what a relief it is for me now knowing I can take her to the dog park and not have to worry about her getting preggers because I missed the onset of her going into heat ever again. It's so nice of you to make a follow-up call. Please give my best to Dr. Goatt and tell him Edie says, hello, too."

"I will, Ms. Abjian. Thank you for your time."

Tom popped into her office as she hung up with Ms. Abjian.

"Thomasina Kiley?" he asked. "I just got a call from Dr. Goatt's receptionist saying she was so sorry to have put me in the office records as Tom Kiley and that she had checked carefully, but couldn't find any evidence Harry Kiley had been neutered by Dr. Goatt or that I had ever been billed for a procedure. She hoped that information would help with my pet insurance mess. Do you know what she's talking about? What am I saying. Of course you know what she means, Thomasina."

"Guilty as charged." Regan walked to the whiteboard and erased the question mark under Dr. Goatt's name in the opportunity/trust box. "I just proved Dr. Goatt's alibi for the time of Judi's murder is good. I was so sure he was the culprit. Solving this crime is going to be harder than I thought."

🏠🏠🏠🏠🏠🏠🏠🏠🏠🏠🏠

Yesterday was such a high playing detective, Regan thought, *today not so much.* It was the second week of her ad campaign in *The Carmel Pine Cone,* so two ads ran, one in the main part of the paper and the second near the Sandy Claws column. She expected results, but as Friday wound down, she realized the paper had been out for a day, not counting the Thursday night release to on-line subscribers, and she had yet to receive a phone call about either of her ads. Her week was a bust: no breaking Dr. Goatt's alibi and no response to her ad trying to find Mireya's half-brother. She felt completely stymied.

She had a Saturday filled with house showings and hopefully offer writing and presenting, and a Sunday morning of offer reviewing with out-of-town owners who were making a special trip to Santa Cruz to consider the nine offers scheduled to be presented on their popular beach house listing. Her weekend promised to be full and action packed and not related to murder or missing persons. She could hardly wait.

Regan was just picking up her purse to head home on Friday night when her office phone rang.

"I'm Angela Pardini. I think you knew my mother-in-law, Judi. My husband, Mike, and I are in town, staying at her condo clearing things out and getting it ready to sell. We found your business card among some notes she must have written just before...I know selling can be a problem when," she made her voice almost inaudible, as if whispering her words could lessen their impact, "something awful has happened in a home."

Regan had a remembered vision of Judi dead in her bed as her daughter-in-law continued rambling amid hesitations and pauses.

"There was an agent from Carmel who stopped by earlier...she said she'd list the condo...even though she knew a murder had happened here...since she's listing Mom Judi's friend's condo. We'd rather have a local agent and someone who knew Mom Judi selling it. We were hoping you could do it...but you were the one who found her, weren't you...so we'll understand if you don't want to."

It took a minute before Regan found her voice. When she did, she forced it to be even and slightly upbeat. "I'd be happy to help. How long will you be staying in Capitola?"

"We're going home late Sunday. We both have to be at work on Monday."

"My day is completely booked tomorrow and on Sunday until at least 1:00, but I could come by around 2:00, if that works for you."

"Perfect."

As Regan hung up, she wondered if what she had just agreed to was perfect or if it might prove to be a perfect nightmare.

She spent time after dinner preparing a portfolio of comparable sales to show the Pardinis and then she pushed the thought of returning to Judi's condo and the final image of what she saw there out of her mind.

🏠🏠🏠🏠🏠🏠🏠🏠🏠🏠🏠

Their meeting on Sunday at the front door of Judi's condo was as fraught as Regan feared it might be. Her slightly awkward, "I'm so sorry about your mother," sounded perfunctory and insincere to her ears, even when she shook Mike Pardini's hand and added personal words: "she was a fighter and a real pal to those who were lucky enough to call her their friend."

"Thank you. Come in, come in," Mike invited.

Regan noted the animal urns were gone, and as they walked toward the kitchen, to her relief she saw Judi's bed was gone, as well.

She must have hesitated as she glanced into the bedroom because Mike announced, "We got rid of Mom's bedroom furniture first thing. We took all her pets, too. Mom wanted their ashes to be scattered with hers. We're not doing the actual dump," he looked horrified at his word choice, "we hired someone with a plane to do that, to scatter them all together over the ocean."

"That would have pleased her, I'm sure."

Regan was relieved when their conversation turned to business and contract signing. She offered to hire a cleaner to finish up and promised she would handle staging the condo.

"So that's it?" Angela asked. "We don't ever have to come back here? Thank you so much; being here has been so much harder than we thought it would be."

The evening was perfect for sitting outside while they waited for Tom's grilled chicken to finish cooking. Its savory aroma was carried on the light breeze off the ocean that made the heatwave Santa Cruz was experiencing tolerable. Tom was animated, happy to be home with his wife and anticipated an evening of doing nothing after a busy week.

"You had quite a successful weekend," he congratulated as he handed her a glass of wine. "One listing in escrow, one set of buyers in contract for a new home, and now another listing. Keep it up and I may have to give you a raise."

"From my perspective, this weekend — this whole week — has been a letdown. I was so sure Dr. Goatt was a killer and that the police just hadn't tried hard enough to break his alibi, but I was wrong about him. Now I understand why the authorities are stuck solving Martha and Judi's murder, because I am, too.

"And I was certain that by now I'd have a great lead on Mireya's brother; instead, I haven't had any results from the ad in *The Carmel Pine Cone*. Even the new listing; it's Judi's condo. So instead of bringing me the excitement and pleasure of devising a great marketing package, all it does is remind me of bad memories. I don't want to set foot in it."

"You're allowed until the chicken is ready to feel disappointed, but after that, I'll expect you to have a new plan and be ready to go to work on it."

"A new plan," Regan scoffed.

"I'll help by doing the staging and office and Brokers' Tour for Judi's condo so you can avoid being around it as much as possible. Why don't you take a couple of days off and get away from everything related to Varner women, too."

"Because having time on my hands is going to make me feel worse, not better." Regan looked at her husband, "Although I guess I could..." She tapped a finger on her lips.

Tom was grinning.

"I think I'll go to Carmel tomorrow. If memory serves, there's a resale store run by the Monterey SPCA near the Barnyard Shopping Center. I saw a sign for it when I drove up Carmel Valley Road trying to find the nonexistent Rancho Grande Village. If the Monterey SPCA is anything like our local group, it's staffed by volunteers, people who probably know all about local dog clubs and breeders. Maybe I was mistaken about how many people read *The Carmel Pine Cone*. Maybe if I talk to live people…"

Tom's grin had grown into a full-fledged smile. "I think dinner's ready," he said.

🏠🏠🏠🏠🏠🏠🏠🏠🏠🏠🏠

The SPCA Benefits Shop in Carmel was just what Regan expected. Like the Grey Bears Thrift Store in Santa Cruz which benefitted seniors, it was stuffed with donated furniture, objects both beautiful and quirky, gently-used clothing, and plants; except the items in the store were Carmel donations and, therefore, most things were considerably upmarket from what might be found in the Santa Cruz resale store.

The volunteers, most of them older, looked more upscale, too. They were easy to spot because of the tidy matching aprons they wore and because many of them had conservatively done manicures with red-tipped nails still popular with their generation and most had hair color which suggested it came from expensive salons, rather than tint boxes found in drugstores.

The volunteers may have differed from Santa Cruz helpers — who often seemed to have an aged San Francisco flower children vibe about them — in style, but not in personality. They were a friendly group on the whole, who were happy to talk to customers.

Regan hoped they were also willing to gossip. She found a huddle of three who weren't busy and approached them.

"You have a wonderful store here. This is my first visit, but it certainly won't be my last. I bet you raise a great deal of money here for the Monterey SPCA."

The shortest of the three offered, "We do our best."

"She's being modest. We almost beat the 'Wag n' Walk' fundraiser last year. This year we hope to, although the proceeds from that event grow every year."

"I know it's a big event," Regan said. "I'm from Santa Cruz, and a friend of mine who was very active in the Santa Cruz SPCA attended last year's walk to see how it all worked because we may try to copy you and have our own version."

"Oh, who was that? I met someone from Santa Cruz at the start of the walk who said she was checking us out. I don't remember her name, but I might, if you say it."

"Her name was Martha Varner."

"Yes! Yes, that's the woman I met." The volunteer's pudgy pink cheeks glowed with her pleased recognition.

The third volunteer, who hadn't said anything to that point, asked, "You keep talking about her in the past tense. Has something happened to her?"

"You're very observant," Regan answered. "And unfortunately, very perceptive. She died earlier this year."

"Oh dear. She was so nice," the pudgy volunteer said. Her cheeks seemed to deflate as she spoke.

Regan agreed. "Yes, she was. Martha, of course, had her dog with her for the walk and she met a man at the 'Wag n' Walk' who had a dog that looked just like her's. After the walk they went for tea at Doris Day's hotel and, while talking, discovered they were related. Martha's husband preceded her in death and her only daughter and grandson

142

don't have much family. They would love to meet the man Martha met on the walk.

"We've been running an ad in *The Carmel Pine Cone* hoping he'd see it — or someone who knew him would — but there's been no response."

"Oh yes," the short volunteer said. "I saw the ad, but I didn't call the number because I didn't have any suggestions as to who he might be."

"What kind of dog does, did, she have?" the reserved woman asked.

"A Chevalier King Charles Spaniel," Regan replied.

"Oh, they're such cute little things, but that's an unusual dog for a man to have. You know they were bred to be ladies' lap dogs," the small volunteer offered.

The taciturn volunteer was concentrating hard. "Very unusual. Bitch or dog?" she asked.

"I'm not sure, but the King Charles Martha and her pet met may have been named 'Queeny,' so that sounds like a female to me," Regan guessed.

"Color?" the matter-of-fact volunteer quizzed.

"Martha's dog is a Blenheim, so since the dogs were similar, I'd would guess the man's dog is, as well."

Volunteer heads started shaking one after the other.

"Doesn't ring any bells. I know of a smattering of Chevalier King Charles pups, Blenheim, too, but they all belong to women and none of them are named 'Queeny'."

"My neighbor has a Chevalier King Charles Spaniel. She knows every dog of that breed in the community. Do you have a card or something with a phone number on it? I'll ask her if she can think of any men who own Chevalier King Charles Spaniels and let you know."

"I do," Regan said as she reached into her purse and produced one of her real estate cards.

"Oh, you're a real estate broker. We know lots of local brokers because so many of them volunteer with us," the pink cheeked woman said, regaining her color.

"Good point, Abbie. You just reminded me of two brokers who have Chevalier King Charles pups. Perhaps they might know of other owners. Let's see," she looked up and touched her hair, deep in thought. "There's Helen Morgan and, oh what's the name of the other one, she's very active at fundraising events, oh, you know who I mean," she sought help from her fellow volunteers. "She's tall and rather striking. She has a sort of man's name, two men's names."

"Do you mean Roya?" the petite volunteer asked.

The two remaining volunteers jumped in at the same time.

"Roya Matthews," they chirped in unison.

"I know her," the rosy cheeked volunteer gushed. "Do you want me to ask her if she knows the man?"

"I know her, too," Regan forced a half-hearted smile. "I'll ask her myself."

As Regan backed her car out of its space near the SPCA Benefit store, her mood was dark. She carried out a conversation with herself, hoping her alter-ego might come up with an escape for her. "Not Roya Matthews again," she groaned. "Couldn't I have a nice day in Carmel playing sleuth without her name coming up? Now I suppose I'll have to go ask her if she knows who Mireya's brother is." No alternative suggestion was forthcoming. "At least I can have lunch before I have to go see her."

Regan decided on The Cypress Inn, which was known locally as Doris Day's Hotel. The actress was renown for her love of animals and her hotel was pet-friendly. Dogs, both as visitors and overnight guests, were as welcome as humans.

On other trips to Carmel, she and Tom had stopped by for a late afternoon drink in the lounge or grand reception room and enjoyed watching patrons meet friends and their dogs. As much as they enjoyed observing, they always felt slightly unsociable without a pet companion.

Theoretically, the Cypress Inn welcomed cats, as well as dogs, so they considered bringing their cat, Harry, with them, but they had only seen one feline in the hotel, a tense little grey tabby who cowered in a baby carriage that her owner used to transport her, terrified of the surrounding sea of dogs. After watching the cat and imagining how Harry would react, Tom and Regan decided they could tolerate being considered anti-pet and that Harry would be grateful they left him at home.

Regan handed the menu back to her server, "I'll have the Portobello mushroom and iced tea. Thank you," she said.

Left alone once again, she eyed the lounge filled with regulars having lunch at the small tables where drinks were served later in the day, hoping luck would be with her and she'd spot a Chevalier King Charles Spaniel nestled at the feet of a male owner. Unfortunately, luck wasn't having lunch at The Cypress.

She smiled at anyone sitting alone who met her gaze, hoping to start a conversation with them. Most smiled back, noticed the absence of a furry critter at her feet, and turned their attention to their pet.

Her server brought her lunch quickly. "Is there anything else I can get for you?" her server asked, the obligatory question that came with the meal.

"Nothing to eat or drink," Regan answered, "but perhaps you could answer a question or two for me. Do you notice the dogs people bring here?"

"Notice?" the server asked. "Well, I notice you don't have a dog with you so, while I, of course, love," she emphasized the word, "dogs, especially since I want to continue working here where the tips are usually good, I assume I can ask exactly what you mean by notice them without offending you.

"So, do you mean notice them like when one of them trips me when I'm carrying a full tray of dishes, or notice them like when their owner leaves a skimpy tip, or worse yet none at all, because I didn't gush about their darling 'animal companion' enough?"

The young woman server laughed. She had mastered putting a light tinkling sound in her voice so it didn't sound as bitter as her words.

"Neither of those things," Regan laughed, too, with genuine amusement. "But I bet you're just the right person to notice the dogs and the people who come in here, especially if they're an unusual combination."

"You mean like the ninety-pound woman with a Mastiff, of the ex-football player with a pocket-sized Chihuahua?"

146

"Exactly. I'm trying to find a man with a Chevalier King Charles Spaniel."

The server pouched out her lips. "Umm, there are half a dozen women regulars who come in here with their big-eyed Chevalier King Charles doggies, but I've never seen a man with one. Sorry."

Regan tried to eat slowly, but in the end, feeling alone and conspicuous, she gobbled her lunch, which was quite tasty, paid her bill, and left a large tip. Then she steeled herself for her upcoming chat with Roya Matthews.

She pulled in front of Roya's real estate office just as a car pulled away from the curb. That wasn't the kind of luck she wanted. She parked in the vacated space, fed the meter, and then straightened her back until her posture was perfect before she walked into the office.

An efficient receptionist asked which agent Regan would like to see.

"Roya Matthews. Please."

"She's away from the office today. May I have her assistant help you?"

Regan started to say no, but changed her mind. "Yes. That would be fine."

The receptionist pressed a button, spoke a few words, and within seconds a woman, as austere as Roya was showy, came out to greet her. The woman was dressed in shades of dark charcoal and black, with a crisp white collar peeking out at her cloistered neckline. The wrist of the hand she extended for Regan to shake was devoid of jewelry.

"Good afternoon. I'm Sally Lyngston, Roya's assistant. How may I help you?" she asked from lips colored by the palest shade of pink lipstick.

"I'm Regan McHenry. Roya and I have met in a business capacity before — I'm a real estate agent, too — but I came by today to ask her a completely non-real estate related question."

"I may not be able to help you then, but I'll do my best. What was it you wished to ask Roya about?"

"I wanted to ask her about her dog. Well, not her dog exactly; I've been told she has a Chevalier King Charles Spaniel."

"You mean Sammy? Yes, she does."

"I'm trying to track down a man who owns a dog like hers, like Sammy, and I thought she might know other owners of that breed."

"I'm afraid that's not something I can help you with. Excuse me? Did you say your name was Regan McHenry? Are you from Santa Cruz?"

"Yes."

"What a coincidence that you should be here when Roya is in Santa Cruz today. She's checking on her two new listings up there. Shall I ask her to call you? I believe she wanted to speak with you about the listings, anyway, so you can ask about dogs when you talk to her."

By the time Regan returned to her car, she was if not angry, at least perturbed. Wouldn't it be just like Roya Matthews to ask her for listing advice for properties in her home town because golden girl Roya didn't know the area well and didn't want to spend the time necessary to educate herself?

Her drive home wasn't a happy one. She'd spent another day chasing after hoped-for leads, if not to murder, at least to Mireya's brother's identity and had gotten nowhere. There was an accident on Highway 1 near Moss Landing that backed traffic up for miles. With no alternative routes available, her anticipated little-over-an-hour trip turned into a two-and-a-half-hour marathon.

She almost went straight home, but realized when she got back to Santa Cruz that it was early enough that Tom would still be at work. So she stopped by the office, prepared to complain to him in the hope of hearing sympathetic noises from her husband.

Instead of finding consolation, she found Roya Matthews ensconced in his office, sitting on his sofa sipping coffee, and laughing at something Tom just told her as if he were the wittiest man on the planet. Of course, Roya looked perfect as always — today's metallic outfit was shimmering silver set off with turquoise jewelry and scarf and very becoming — must she also be an accomplished coquette?

"Sweetheart!" Tom rose abruptly from his end of the sofa and gave her a quick peck on the cheek. "Your timing is perfect. We were about to sign a referral agreement for the Varner condo and house."

Roya smiled up at Regan, "Yes. I really don't have time to service the listings properly because I'm swamped with listings closer to home. And admittedly, I don't know the market here as well as Kiley and Associates does, so I'll just take twenty-percent and turn things over to you. I know twenty-five is more customary, but we're all friends here and I do appreciate that you've must feel a wee bit upset that I have the listings, since you've done business with both Martha and her daughter in the past."

"I wouldn't worry about that, Roya. Like you said, Martha preferred you. And I do have plenty to do, as well," Regan said.

"Regan listed another property near Martha Varner's condo just yesterday," Tom offered, "so we'll take advantage of that to do some double marketing on them."

"What a good idea," Roya cooed.

"I understand you talked to the sellers about the condo I listed. The Pardinis?" Regan asked.

"Why yes, I did. Evidently, they liked you better than me, though," Roya chuckled, finding her statement quite clever, "so things worked out. Do you think the condos will be difficult to sell, given their history?"

"No, I don't think so," Tom said. "I suspect young techies from over the hill will snap them up for weekend beach getaways. Anything within walking distance to the beach is selling well and the condos make ideal vacation getaways."

"I imagine you'll word your advertising so well," Roya giggled charmingly, "you'll have them thinking owning a property where a murder was committed is exciting or a great story to tell their friends. You're such an ingenious man."

Regan thought her husband blushed just a bit.

"Before you go, Roya, I did want to ask you a question about dogs," Regan chimed in.

"Dogs?"

"Yes, dogs. As it turns out, I spent the day in Carmel playing detective. Before she died, Martha Varner may have discovered a," Regan hesitated; she didn't want to say a child given up for adoption since that was more private information than Roya needed to know, "an estranged relative who supposedly lives in the Carmel area and owns a Chevalier King Charles Spaniel named Queeny.

"I put an ad in *The Carmel Pine Cone* asking for information, but didn't get any responses. So today I went to the SPCA Benefits store and asked around. Your name came up as a possible resource, since you know so many people in the area and own a dog like Martha's."

Roya played with her scarf. "I do have a King Charles."

"I know. I stopped by your office and your assistant said you did. The missing relative is a man; would you know anyone who fits that description?"

"I can't think of anyone. Queeny is the dog's name, you said?"

"That's not for certain. But the relative being a man is."

"No. I'm sorry. I can't think of any men like the one you're looking for."

Roya uncrossed her long legs and stood up. "Well, Tom, darling, do you have those papers ready for me to sign? I need to get back to Carmel. I have a function to attend tonight."

Roya teetered across the room to Tom's desk on silvery stiletto heels — the highest Regan had ever seen anyone wear — stooped, and quickly signed the paperwork he had waiting for her.

"I'm off, then," she announced, as she checked her scarf for slippage and gave it a theatrical toss over her shoulder as she left Tom's office.

"Whew," Tom said, "one-on-one she's somewhat overwhelming."

"Admit it, 'Tom darling,' you like her."

"I find her interesting. She's probably a bit shady, but highly entertaining. And she flirts with me. Any time an attractive woman does that, even if it's an obvious tool she uses to ease business along, it's flattering. Then there's the fact that she brings out a bit of the green-eyed-monster in you, which is doubly entertaining. Her flirting bothers you, which reminds me that you love me," he laughed.

Regan was in a sour mood the next morning, her outlook not helped because Tom was gone before she woke, not for a golf game, but to prepare for the quarterly Broker's Breakfast that it was his turn to chair. She had missed wishing him well and felt remorse because he was probably going to need all the moral support he could get. The topic for the day's meeting was the impact of Airbnb on rentals and neighborhoods. It was a hot issue in Santa Cruz, with the community split between property rights proponents and supporters of affordable rentals. If the meeting was anything like the last Board of Supervisor's meeting, Tom was going to have his hands full keeping the opinionated brokers on good terms.

When her office phone rang at 9:30, she picked it up quickly, without noting the caller ID because she expected it to be him, wounded, exhausted, and seeking the comfort of her voice. "Poor baby. Is your head still firmly attached?" she asked by way of a hello.

"I believe it is," the voice of a mystified female responded.

"Oh, I'm so sorry. I thought you were someone else," Regan apologized.

"Obviously. Are you waiting for a call? Should I call back later?" the woman asked.

"No, no. This is a good time for us to talk," Regan said, trying not to sound too sheepish.

"We met at the SPCA Benefits Store in Carmel yesterday," the woman said. "I'm the one who has the neighbor who knows everything there is to know about local Chevalier King Charles Spaniels and their owners. Do you remember me?"

"Yes, I do." Regan perked up at the possibility of getting a lead to Mireya's brother; she smiled hopefully.

"Well, I asked her if she knew of any dogs with male owners who live in the area. I'm afraid she doesn't."

Regan's smile dissolved.

"She did remember one man with a Blenheim colored dog like that, though, who spent several months here, but she said he hasn't been in town in ages. He came here to look at property, oh, she thought it must have been four or five years ago, but you know how time passes. What seems like three or four years all of a sudden becomes six or seven, especially as you get older — maybe you're not old enough for that to happen to you yet — and she's definitely older."

Regan could hardly contain her question until the woman finished speaking. "Does she remember his name?"

"I asked her that. Unfortunately, she doesn't. All she remembers is that he was an architect, a very successful one she thinks, from somewhere back East and, of course, she remembers his dog."

Regan's hand shook as she hung up the phone. It was a leap, certainly, but she didn't think it was a big one. There was an architect from back East who was looking to buy property in Carmel a few years ago who had a dog like Martha's. Couple that with the fact that Martha entered into a purchase contract with a back East architect shortly after she met a man with a dog like her's at the Monterey SPCA Walk who she believed was her long-lost son. It all seemed too tidy to be a random occurrence. In her mind, Regan would consider that anyone betting against the owner/architect Martha bought the property in Rancho Grande Village from being her long-lost son was going to lose their money.

Regan retrieved her copy of Martha Varner's purchase contract and found the architect's name. Mathius Royce Hugel. Regan typed the name into her computer. Several page listings popped up; she selected the one that looked like his personal webpage. She wasn't rewarded with a photo of the architect, just several of his designs. There were exterior photos of homes and their city locations, but very little else.

As she scrolled down the page in search of additional information, she noticed the copyright date for the page was seven years old. A quick search for updates indicated the page hadn't been updated for almost that long.

She moved to another of the pages on the search list. After reviewing most of the remaining options, Regan realized all indications were that Mathius Royce Hugel hadn't been active online for several years.

She turned her attention to the acronym for the architectural group listed after his name and typed in NAAB. She expected to find something akin to the National

Association of Realtors page where she might be able to put in his name and be rewarded with his location and license number, but she was disappointed to find there was no master list equivalent on the site.

There was one person who should know where he was and how to contact him, however: Roya Matthews. She was the listing agent for his property and he had assigned power of attorney to her for his real estate dealings.

Regan pulled Roya's business card off the folder. She turned it over and over, as if looking at it from another angle might give her insight into Roya's thought process as she considered what to do.

Had Martha started working with Roya at her son's suggestion because she had his property listed? That certainly seemed like the correct order of business, and if it was, Roya must have known about the connection because, given the way clients talk to their real estate agents, surely Martha or her son, or possibly both, would have mentioned it at some point. So why, when Roya knew the search was on for Martha Varner's son, hadn't she said she knew who he was? Would she cite client privacy again? If she did, was it something she believed or just a handy way of ignoring what Regan was asking?

Regan was sure that Roya knew more than she let on and Regan wanted to know what Roya knew. It seemed a confrontation was in order. The only question for her was did she want to watch Roya as she asked her questions — body language could be so telling to an able observer like she was — or was hearing Roya over the phone good enough.

It didn't take her long to decide she wanted to see Roya's reactions; it took her even less time to decide she needed Tom's participation with Roya's interview.

Tom was enthused about Ambrosia in Scotts Valley, a new-to-him restaurant a golfing buddy had taken him to for lunch when they finished a round at Pasatiempo Golf Course. He had insisted Regan meet him there for dinner so he could introduce her to the delights of Indian cuisine, something she hadn't yet tried.

He rose, not to his full height, but enough to demonstrate respect, when she approached his table. It was such an old-fashioned gesture and Tom was such a modern man, that his action made her fall a little bit more in love with him every time he did it. Regan leaned forward and gave him a quick peck on his cheek before they both sat down.

As the samosas avocado chat that Tom had ordered for starters arrived, Regan made an unexpected request of him. "I want you to come with me to Carmel tomorrow to meet with Roya Mathews and I want you to flirt with her like crazy."

"Excuse me?" He dropped his samosa on the tiny plate in front of him. "You want me to flirt with her?"

"Shamelessly."

"But I thought…"

"I don't like it that you find her attractive and I don't like it that she flirts with you even in front of me, but I need you to play along with her. Make her feel comfortable, in control, and maybe even a little cocky, so I can catch her off balance."

He shook his head, mystified by his wife.

"Even though I may be almost a tiny bit jealous of her," Regan squirmed in her seat, "I know she's not a threat to us. You still get up for me," she smiled seductively at her husband, "which means you still love me."

"More than I could ever love anyone else."

Regan asked Tom to set up the meeting in Roya Matthew's office using the pretext of reviewing advertising material, something that could easily be done online, but at Regan's behest, he said he was looking forward to seeing her again, mixing business with pleasure, and drinking the something stronger she offered the last time he was in her office. He didn't mention Regan was coming, too.

Tom poked his head in her office and offered a single word: "Done."

"Wait, wait," Regan called after him as his head disappeared. "How did she sound?"

His entire body came into her office. "Does it matter?"

"Well, yes, I mean, no," she waffled. "You're enjoying this, aren't you?"

"Oh, yes," he offered a devilish grin. "We better get going. It's the start of Car Week in Carmel and roads may be clogged with tourists. We wouldn't want to be late and keep Roya waiting."

Regan grabbed her purse and headed for her office door. "Coming."

Tom watched her appreciatively as she moved toward him. "By the way, you look especially lovely today. You have more pink in your cheeks than usual, and you're wearing that tight green dress I like so much because it shows off your figure and makes your hazel eyes seem green, too. Subterfuge suits you.

"What is it exactly that you want me to do," Tom asked as he maneuvered his car out of the Kiley and Associates parking lot toward Mission Street.

"Just be yourself, but be receptive to Roya's attention. I think she enjoys being noticed by attractive men, especially in front of other women. If I used what I learned with my behavioral science degree, I could probably come up with a pretty interesting psychological profile of what her insecurities are to explain why she acts the way she does."

"But you don't like her, do you, I mean beyond you thinking she's flirting with me."

"I still think she took advantage of Martha to make a sale, so no, I don't particularly like her. But I dislike her even more because I'm certain she knows that her client is Martha's long-lost son and she won't put him in touch with his sister."

"Have you considered that it may not be Roya who's unwilling to move contact forward? From what you've told me about your search for him online, he sounds like he's made some effort to become invisible. He sounds like a very private person. Roya may have told him — Martha's son, if you're right — about Mireya and he may be the one who doesn't want a half-sister in his life."

Tom's question gave Regan pause if only for a few seconds. "Well, then that's something else I need to ask her, isn't it?'

Carmel was more than a little overrun with tourists. People meandered across streets, in and out of crossing spaces and backed up cars that couldn't move forward for fear of hitting one of them. Parking was nonexistent. Fortunately, Roya's office had its own lot, which, while small, had two vacant spaces available when they managed to reach it.

Even having allowed for a slowdown, they were fifteen minutes late for their appointment. When they were announced, a forgiving Roya came from her office with a smile on her face and a hand extended warmly toward Tom.

"You poor darling. I know what this week is like; I should have volunteered to come to you," she cooed, a vision in glacial white laced with enough crystalline silver threads that she shimmered coolly as she moved. Her ever-present scarf was made of the same material, and it glistened, as well. "Oh, and Regan, you're here, too. How nice," she added pleasantly enough while still placing Regan firmly as an afterthought in her greeting.

Roya looped her arm through Tom's and pulled him forward. "Let's get that drink I promised."

Tom started their conversation with flattery. "You know, not every woman can pull it off, but you look good wearing white, Roya."

Roya twittered, "Barely. I go to Cabo every three months to maintain my tan and I'm overdue. I'm so faded, I hoped wearing white might make me seem more bronzed, give me a bit of a glow for you."

"It definitely worked."

Regan was left to follow them like an embodied addendum to the meeting and, she suspected, exactly the role Roya planned for her.

They were shown to a long sofa in Roya's office and assigned to sit on it.

"Leave space for me so I can see your advertising material," Roya instructed. "Tom, you look like a single-malt man to me."

"How did you know?' he asked.

"Most big strong men seem to appreciate good Scotch. Neat or with ice?" she chortled.

"Neat."

"Besides, with your devastatingly blue eyes, I bet you have a bit of Scotsman in you, am I right?"

"A bit, on my mother's side."

She handed him a generous pour.

"Regan, what would you like?"

"Just coffee, thank you."

"Let me at least make it Irish for you." Roya said, doctoring Regan's drink without waiting for her acceptance of the offer.

She poured Scotch over ice for herself — a much smaller amount than she gave Tom — and squeezed onto the sofa between him and his end of it.

"Let's see what you have for me," she said, as she crossed her legs, brushed his ankle with her foot, and aligned her hip against his.

As Tom showed her advertising materials from his laptop, Roya maneuvered so she could smile up into his face. "Oh, you are good, but then I expected you would be," she offered coquettishly.

Tom played his part well, smiling back appreciatively and leaning toward Roya to illustrate a point. He even brushed Roya's leg with the back of his hand as he adjusted the laptop so she could have a better view.

Roya giggled — yes, giggled — Regan noted with disgust, as Tom spoke and he responded with flattered chuckles.

Regan had instructed him to display prurient interest if Roya encouraged him, but when she did and he did, Regan found herself having to fight the green-eyed monster rising within her. She consoled herself that Tom's behavior was part of a pre-planned act. Still, it was hard for her to know if, when she decided the time was right for her question it was because she was sure it was, or because she simply couldn't watch Roya with her husband any longer.

"Roya, when did you know your client Mathius Hugel and Mireya Varner were half siblings?" she asked casually.

Roya Matthews fell silent. She touched her trademark scarf and opened and closed her mouth more than once without uttering a sound. Regan was glad she was able to see Roya's reaction because the magnitude of it wouldn't have been apparent over the phone.

As obviously shaken as she had been by Regan's question, Roya maintained icy control when she finally did utter her first words. "I knew Martha Varner was Mathius' mother before I met her. When I did meet her, Martha told me she had another…child, so their relationship wasn't hard to figure out."

"If you knew, why didn't you say something when you knew Mireya was trying to contact him?"

"I've known Mathius for ever — we're even distantly related — and we're very close. I know his history and even though he had wonderful adoptive parents, I know how hard it was for him knowing he had been rejected by his mother. Why should I help his half-sister, his mother's offspring, find him? Who knows how painful it would have been for him to meet a woman who had everything he missed growing up?"

Regan frowned, "But, Mireya wasn't responsible for…"

Tom interrupted her. "Did you tell him about Mireya?"

"He knew about her."

"Did you tell him she wanted to meet him?" Regan queried, "or did you decide he didn't need to know that by yourself?"

Roya's eyes flashed anger. "Mathius, Mireya, Martha. Their connections are none of your concern, Regan. And I've had just about enough of you butting in to my life and business on behalf of Mireya Varner." Roya's voice became cold and menacing. "I can speak for Mathius; we are of the same mind.

"Now I want you to get out of my office and to stop bothering me on behalf of that woman. All our business dealings are to be handled in a professional manner. Tom, in future, consult my broker. He will relay anything I need to know to me. Is that clear?"

Roya rose disentangling herself from Tom in a manner that emphasized she no longer found him delightful and sat down at her desk, using it to put an additional barrier between her and them. Then she busied herself with papers she found on it as if Regan and Tom had already left her office.

"I guess we've been told," Tom said a bit sheepishly when they were back in his car. "And from her perspective, we have been challenging her: first her ethics and now her candor."

"You mean I've been challenging her." Regan put her finger to her mouth absentmindedly chewing on a fingernail. "I had other questions I wanted to ask her. And the way she reacted just now, I'm not ready to stop looking for answers."

"I am," he said firmly, "and I want you to stop, too. Mireya has moved to Canada. She's building a family there; she doesn't need a brother with baggage who may or may not want to be in her life, and any ethical questions you have about Roya Matthews conduct with Martha Varner's contract would be hard to prove. Let it go, Sweetheart."

Regan tilted her head just a bit and glanced at him out of the corner of her eye.

"I mean it, Regan. I want you to promise me you're done with Roya Matthews and Mathias Hugel. In fact, I wish you'd stop thinking about anything to do with Varners."

She sighed theatrically. "With Roya and Mr. Hugel, Okay. But don't ask me to stop trying to find out who killed Martha and Judi."

Tom nodded his acquiesces. He knew it was a waste of effort to try for more concessions from his wife.

14

Even though she wanted to, Regan found it impossible to stop wondering about Mathius Hugel. He had seemingly disappeared and yet he was still actively present as recently as the Monterey SPCA fundraiser walk. Was he living locally or had he gone back East?

He had given power of attorney to Roya Matthews, she said to make his transaction easier, but it wasn't clear if that happened some time ago or after the fundraiser. If it was recent, did that mean that he had become incapacitated? Probably not. Not if he had created plans for housing for Mireya and Martha and possibly himself, too. His plans were detailed and complete. Such effort would require sharp mental faculties and their drawing should have been physically demanding, as well.

What did he know about Mireya? How was he handling his mother's murder? The wondering didn't keep Regan up at night, but it popped into her mind at odd times.

It didn't intrude on her thoughts at the open house she was holding in Martha's condo, however. Tom was holding an open house in Judi's condo and a flood of potential buyers were moving between the proximate properties. All the activity left her no time to ponder.

"Darn. You're not her either," a clearly annoyed voice rang out from the condo doorway. It belonged to a tall, rail-thin speaker with a grey sensible pageboy hairdo who came inside and up so close to Regan that her personal space felt breached.

Regan reflexively took a step backward before offering the complainer a quizzical smile. "Who am I not?"

"That real estate agent. There's a man in Judi's condo and here you are at Martha's. I expected that the real estate agent I talked to outside of Judi's place about listing my condo would be here somewhere. She said she was going to be listing Martha's condo and would be happy to add my home to her list, although she told me if I could hold off just a bit, it would be beneficial because, with two murders here, buyers might be anxious, and the value of my condo might be depressed because of that. She said if I could just stay put for a few months, I'd get a higher price. I wanted to talk to her about that, but she's not here, or there, or anywhere."

"She's right," Regan launched into real estate speak, "the recent history here could affect prices in the entire building."

"I wanted to speak with her. I'm sure you and that man at Judi's know your stuff, but the agent I talked to, well, she was so impressive. Forceful, and a real head turner, if you know what I mean. Do you know how I can reach her?"

"Did she give you, her name?" Regan asked for a name, even though she was sure who the impressive-looking agent was.

"She did, but I forget it. I was sure I'd remember it because it was something out of the ordinary, but I don't."

"Roya Matthews?" Regan suggested.

"That's it! That's her name."

"She's based in Carmel and has turned the listing of Martha's condo over to me and my husband — he's the man you met — and we've listed Judi's condo, as well. You probably caught her the day she came up to inspect Martha's condo, but Roya Matthews won't be coming back up here again. Sorry."

"I know I don't have her," Regan searched for a word that wasn't negative, "charisma, but I'll be happy to meet with you to discuss your property, if you like. I'm Regan McHenry, by the way," Regan said as she extended her hand.

"Madeline Stichman." The woman touched Regan's hand with three of her fingers in an insipid handshake. "I guess you'll do. Could you come by when you finish here? I'm upstairs, right above Judi."

"I'll be happy to. This open house is over at four. I'll come up as soon as it ends."

Tom took over locking up and sign collecting and agreed to come back to the condo building to pick up Regan when he finished. Regan used the stairs between Martha and Judi's condos to reach Madeline Stichman's condo. The front door opened as she raised her hand to knock.

"Come in. You're prompt. That's a good sign. I've been sitting here thinking about what I said to you. I'm not really such a pain-in-the-neck as I seemed. I've lost two friends, not close ones, but we all lived in this building for several years and ran into one another collecting mail and parking our cars. You know how it is?"

Regan nodded empathetically. "I do. People become part of your life in many ways. When they aren't there any longer, and especially considering how Martha and Judi were taken away, it's difficult."

"Did you know them?" Madeline asked.

"Martha and I were friends. I just met Judi a couple of days before she was killed, but I liked her immediately." Regan decided not to mention she had found Judi's body. "She was coming by my office the day she was murdered."

Madeline frowned. "Was she going to sell her condo, too? Did she want to ask you about selling it?"

"I don't think so. Martha was moving to Carmel and may have hoped Judi would join her there because they were such great friends, but once Martha died, I don't think Judi had any incentive to move. She had nowhere special to go."

"I wonder why she was talking to that real estate agent, then."

"As I said, the Carmel agent was going to be listing Martha's condo. Judi may have run into her there."

"No. The real estate woman was coming out of Judi's condo when I met her. Judi was at the door saying goodbye and the agent said something about looking forward to working with her. Oh, well. Now, come have a look-see around and tell me what I can expect to get from my condo. I imagine it's more valuable than Martha's or Judi's since it's on a higher floor with even better ocean views and didn't have a murder committed in it."

Regan began discussing pricing as Mrs. Stichman showed her around and explained why she might indeed do well to wait until any mention of murders in such close proximity had time to fade when it hit her.

"Mrs. Stichman, when we met at Martha's condo, didn't you say the real estate agent mentioned two murders being committed in this building?"

"Yes, I did."

"And you said she was coming out of Judi's condo when you met her?"

"Correct."

"And Judi was at the door?"

"Yes."

"Did you see or hear Judi talking to the agent?"

"I must have because the real estate agent was talking to her."

"But did you actually see or hear Judi? Or did you just hear what Roya Matthews said to her?"

Madeline Stichman's face revealed confusion. "I...didn't see her...but I must have heard her...because they were conversing. Why? Does it matter?"

"Yes, I think it does. Please think about it carefully," Regan posed her question again. "Did you hear Judi?"

"Probably not," Madeline Stichman said slowly. She inclined her head with her realization. "No, I just heard what that real estate agent said and then she closed Judi's door...oh, that's odd, isn't it? You'd think Judi would have been the one to close her door from the inside, wouldn't you? That's what I would have done in her place."

"It is odd, Mrs. Stichman. This is extremely important: are you absolutely sure the agent said murders, not murder?"

"Oh, no question about it," this time her answer came quickly and with certainty. "She said two murders."

"Did the Capitola police interview you after Judi's murder? Did you tell them what you told me just now?"

"They did come by a few days after Judi was killed. They asked if I had seen anyone, any strange men in particular, lurking around. I hadn't, and I told them so."

"Did you tell them about Roya Matthews?"

"No. I didn't even think to mention the real estate agent because she, well, she was a she, and she had business with Martha and I thought with Judi, so she wasn't a stranger."

"Another listing in the offing?" Tom asked when Regan opened the passenger door to his car and climbed inside.

"I forgot to ask."

"You forgot to ask?"

"It's so important to ask the right questions, isn't it, and that wasn't one of the questions that needed asking. We need to see Dave immediately."

"What's going on, Sweetheart?" Tom asked Regan as he drove, but she didn't offer him an explanation.

"If I start, you'll be…no, wait till we get to Dave's."

By the time they rang Dave and Sandy's doorbell, Tom was almost as agitated as Regan was.

There was no answer, and a frustrated Regan rang the bell again, knocked on the door, and called out, "Dave?"

"I think I smell bar-b-que smoke," Tom said. "I bet they're out on their patio grilling dinner. They can't hear us from there."

Regan smelled smoke, too, and had already started for the side of the house by the time Tom finished speaking. She was thwarted in her attempt to reach the backyard by the high locked side-yard gate that blocked her way.

"Dave? Sandy? Dave, hello!" she yelled. When there wasn't an immediate response, she pounded on the solid gate. "Dave! Dave, I know you're back there." She followed up with, "Daaave!" delivered more as a howl than as a shout.

"You know patience is a virtue, don't you, Regan?" Dave hollered from his side of the tall gate. A moment later it creaked open as he lifted the backyard-side latch and pulled the gate toward him.

He was dressed in one of his usual Hawaiian shirts the body of which was covered by a huge grease-smudged apron with lettering that read: 'I'm the grill master. I burn things for a living. Don't fork with me' and he still had a grill-mitt on his left hand.

"What is your problem, Regan?" He was clearly annoyed at her interrupting his cooking efforts.

"The Capitola police are my problem. They don't know how to interview witnesses and they don't know how to solve murders, and you need to tell them so and get them to do something about it."

"Hi, Dave," Tom waved hello over Regan's shoulder as if his wife and friend weren't having a heated meeting. "May we come in?"

"Is there any way I could stop her," Dave asked Tom sarcastically, as if an overwrought Regan wasn't present, facing him, her hands on her hips. "Do you know what's got her so worked up?"

"She wouldn't say."

"Come on back. I'm smoking meat."

Dave led the way to the backyard with Regan following him closely. She leaned forward and fairly danced after him as she waved her hands beside her like she was trying to shake water off of them.

"I met a woman at an open house today who saw someone leaving Judi's condo after she was killed. The Capitola police didn't even get a description, let alone the name of the person, which my witness had because the killer told it to her."

"Interesting." Dave was nonchalant.

"Dave, I'm serious. I know who killed Martha and Judi. Their neighbor, Mrs. Stichman, told me everything I needed to know to figure it out."

"And do you plan to share that information or keep it secret? What's the name, Regan?

"The name she said was Roya Matthews..."

Tom exploded. "Roya? Stop it, Regan, you're becoming obsessed with that woman!"

"Little annoying fact, Regan. We know the murderer was male," Dave added.

"It wasn't really Roya Matthews, just a man impersonating her."

Tom was speechless.

"Impersonating her? Who would impersonate her and why," Dave asked coldly. He was no longer mocking, but it was hard for Regan to tell if he was irritated and trying to control his temper or settling into the role of police professional.

"Martha Varner had an illegitimate son years ago; she gave him up for adoption. Roya Matthews said she's related to him. I bet there's a family resemblance, although there wouldn't have to be since Mrs. Stichman never saw Roya before the day of Judi's murder, so Martha's son could have just dressed in some of her signature clothing..."

"So, we have a crossdressing-adoptee-murderer, do we?" Dave taunted.

"Yes, I think we do." Now that she had told Dave most of her theory, she had calmed down considerably. She answered him evenly. "I think Martha's son killed her."

"Why?" What's his motive?" Dave's question was delivered with surgical precision.

"My guess is he hated his mother for giving him up."

"Okay, I'll play along. So we got a little mommy don't love me, sob, sob matricide going on here. Why did he kill Judi Pardini, and why did he dress like a woman to do it?"

"He must have thought Martha told Judi something about him — they were best friends, after all — that if she disclosed it, would lead the police to him."

Dave almost snarled. "You didn't answer my question about the cross-dressing part. This guy hinky or something? In your highly-trained opinion, of course."

"Roya Matthews was listing Martha's condo. She would have a reason to be at the building, so I don't think he was cross-dressing or 'hinky' as you call it. He just used her persona as a disguise. Roya has a quite flamboyant signature style. If he was noticed, people who saw him would describe Roya."

"That's right, Dave. Roya Matthews does have a certain, unforgettable style," Tom added.

"So," Regan continued, "dressing like her would be the perfect cover. It appears to have worked, too because Mrs. Stichman spoke to him and still described Roya, whose name he used, and thought he was a woman."

Dave's tone was even, but steely. "Even for you, Regan, this wild concoction you've come up with is too much."

"There's an easy way to prove me right or wrong," Regan dared. "If the murderer is Martha Varner's son, he's Mireya Varner's half-brother. Mireya said the police collected a DNA sample from her before they let her leave the country. Ask the Capitola police to run the DNA sample from Judi's fingernails against Mireya's DNA. Even though you think my idea is farfetched, if there's a familial match, it would prove I'm right."

"And just why are they going to do that test, Regan? I'm pretty sure they won't think just 'cause I have a crazy realtor friend who thinks she's better at solving murders than they are telling them to is a good reason to spend their resources."

"If the Capitola police need convincing to do the test, tell them to re-interview Mrs. Stichman and this time to ask their questions properly."

Tom was quiet for most of the drive home. Finally, he asked, "Do you really believe Mathius Hugel killed his mother because she abandoned him and he hated her for it?"

Regan shrugged. "That's the only explanation for him killing her I could come up with on short notice. I thought about a financial motive, but the way Martha's contract was written, it looks like he got almost everything she had, so that doesn't make sense. "

"If he planned to kill her, why would he have drawn-up property plans that seem to include his living with Mireya and her?"

"I'm not sure. Perhaps to get Martha to go along with him until he had an opportunity to kill her."

"If that was what he wanted to do, he must have had plenty of other opportunities, better opportunities to kill her. Couldn't he have invited her for a walk somewhere secluded and simply murdered her where there were no witnesses? Why wait to kill her at home, where he was more likely to be seen, and why try to make her death appear to be suicide?"

"I'm guessing about his motive for killing Martha; I don't really know why he killed his mother. All I know for sure is that the Roya persona told Mrs. Stichman two murders had been committed before it was public knowledge, which must mean she...or he... knew Judi was dead."

"Isn't it possible Mrs. Stichman met the real Roya coming out of Judi's condo and that she had discovered Judi's body before you did?"

"I guess," Regan said uneasily, "but why not call the police and say so? Why try to cover up the fact that Judi was dead by having an imaginary conversation with her?"

Tom's only reply was a silent headshake.

Both of them were quiet for the next few turns along Empire Grade. Regan was the one to break the silence of their ride. "Tom, the long and short of it is none of this speculating matters. DNA is going to prove me right or wrong; it's as simple as that. If I'm right, motive can come later."

The comparisons were made — Regan wondered if it was hard or easy for Dave to convince the Capitola Police Department to arrange the match-check, but he refused to comment — and the tests proved she was right. Mireya's DNA and the material found under Judi's fingernails showed a familial match, which made it almost certain that Mathius Hugel was Martha Varner's son and that he had probably committed matricide and then killed Judi.

"The lead officer at CPD is interviewing your pal Roya Matthews tomorrow morning, since she's the only connection with Mathius Hugel that we know about," Dave said when he told her about the DNA match.

Regan didn't expect the favor, but decided it couldn't hurt to ask. "Could someone tell me what she has to say…kind of as a reward for me suggesting the DNA test?"

"Seriously? That's a cheeky ask even for you. No way."

"Are you going to be there?"

"Me? No. I don't have any skin in this game. I seem to be just the messenger boy between you, CPD, your little buddy

Mireya, and, well, you'll probably think of more people to bring into this, if I know you."

"But, wouldn't you love to be a fly on the wall?" Regan asked with breathy enthusiasm.

Dave let a "You bet!" slip out before he regained his professional equanimity. "But it's not going to happen."

Regan checked her office clock every few minutes the next morning, distracted from the offers that had come in for Judi's condo following the open house and were being presented later in the day to Judi's son and daughter-in-law. Her imagination overran her professionalism as she envisaged what Roya might be saying to the Capitola officer in charge of her interview and wondering if Dave, with his uncanny way of collecting information from all the law enforcement agencies in the county, would find out what she said.

Regan heard her stomach complain about its lack of lunch by grumbling loudly at a little after 1:30 and was surprised to realize how hungry she was. She started down the hall from her office to Tom's to see if he was there and in the same state when Amanda called out to her from the receptionist desk in a voice that was both formal and keen.

"Regan, I just buzzed Tom. There's a woman here to see both of you."

Regan turned away from his office as Tom emerged, quickly caught up with her, and pressed his hand in the small of her back. "You'll never believe who," was all he managed to say before Regan spotted their visitor.

Roya Matthews was dressed as she had been the first time Regan met her: in gold from head to toe. She stood tall, still, and unsmiling, an Academy Award statuette personified and come to call.

Neither Regan nor Tom were quite sure how to greet her after she had so angrily thrown them out of her office the last time they had seen her.

It was Roya who spoke first, uttering her request in a shaky voice. She held out her hand to Tom, "I need to sit down. And if you have anything stiff to drink, I need a shot of it."

Tom rushed to support her as she wobbled on her stiletto heels. They wound up as a threesome, with Regan to her right and Tom on her left moving slowly down the hallway to Tom's office.

Once there, Roya collapsed on to his sofa with melodramatic flare, adjusted her scarf, and asked with fluttering eyelashes, "Tom, darling, do you have a hankie?"

Regan grabbed a box of tissues off his desk and held it out toward Roya who, when she had pulled out the requisite tissue, dabbed at her eyes gingerly so as not to disturb her makeup.

"I'm so sorry for how I've behaved," she sniffed. Roya fluttered her eyelashes at Tom as he handed her a neat Scotch poured from a bottle he kept in his credenza.

"I never imagined Mathius could have…what it looks like he…" she stuttered and bit her lip. "But the police have such compelling evidence, don't they…that he killed that woman…and now he may have escaped to Mexico, or even worse. It's possible he intends to take his life."

Regan was unsure of how much she and Tom were supposed to know about the missing man and the accusations against him. She also didn't know how to react to the newly vulnerable Roya before her. Did her dislike and distrust of the woman make her question whether the Roya she saw was genuinely as unguarded and upset as she seemed, or giving a performance evocative of her outfit.

"Mathius and I have so much in common. I was a foundling like he was. His adoptive parents accepted me into their home, too, and while they never formally adopted me, they loved both of us equally and raised us together, two peas in a pod. Naturally we were close."

There was a slight quavering in Roya's voice as she went on. "I remember only too well what it was like for Mathius when he was told he was adopted. His adoptive parents told him — showed him — how much they loved him and how glad they were to have him, but I knew how badly it hurt him to know his real parents, especially his mother, gave him away.

"He grew up, we both did, and he got his life in order and became a successful architect, but he had so much he wanted to tell his real mother and wished he could find her." Roya cast her eyes downward and shook her head with sad empathy.

Tom had clearly succumbed to Roya's presentation and, as she continued to speak, Regan began believing she was no longer seeing a performance, as well.

"I know he looked for her for a long time. The state where he was born didn't allow adult children to find information about their birth mother. He hired a private detective, and eventually, he found Martha Varner. He was as excited as a child at Christmas, but circumspect, too. He didn't just go knock on her door or anything like that."

Roya chuckled pitifully. "He moved to Carmel for a time — that was as close to her as he could come at that point in his life. He spent time parked on the street outside her house, but he couldn't face her. And then — it took him several years while he did what he needed to do to get ready for their meeting — the time finally came.

"Mathius did his homework and found out about Martha's involvement with the SPCA and that she was going to the Monterey SPCA Wag n' Walk. He asked to borrow my dog, Sammy, and he worked with him until Sammy responded to the name Queeny — Sammy is a very bright little guy for a Chevalier King Charles Spaniel and a fast learner. Mathius figured Sammy's spare parts wouldn't be noticeable under his long fur, so with Sammy in tow, he sidled up to Martha Varner during the walk, chatted about what a coincidence it was that they both owned Chevalier King Charles Spaniels with the same name, and invited her to have tea after the walk. It was at that tea that he told her who he really was.

"It took so much courage to do that because her reaction to her abandoned child might have been quite different from what it was. Fortunately, she was thrilled to reconnect with her baby.

"I know him so well; he has always been such a gentle man, never a violent one. He would never cause harm to anyone without an overwhelming reason. At some point his mother must have told him something so unbearable it made him snap."

"Did you know he impersonated you when he killed his mother's friend?" Regan asked as gently as she could.

"What? No, he wouldn't do that to me. No, no."

"A witness described you perfectly. Except for the male DNA under Judi's fingernails, you might have been blamed for the murder."

"He did that to me?" Roya's mouth opened and closed as she grasped her scarf and shook her head. "Why would he do something like that to me?"

"Did you tell the police where he is?" Tom asked.

"I couldn't because I don't know. Mathius sent me a note, which arrived this morning before I came up here to be interviewed — it felt like I was being interrogated, not interviewed," Roya rolled her eyes dramatically — "which I gave to the police. He said he was going to Mexico and that he planned to put an end to his existence there once and for all. I'm so afraid for him.

"I know he likes Cancun and Acapulco and the old elegance of Guadalajara; we both do. We've traveled there for years, sometimes together, so I know some mutually favored spots. I'm flying down there tomorrow morning to see if I can find him, starting in Acapulco."

Roya opened her purse and took out an envelope. "I've arranged for someone in my office to cover for me so I can be away for as long as I need to be. I'm passing on my power of attorney to you, Tom, to accept offers on his behalf, together with an outline of acceptable terms. As long as an offer is presented that meets my criteria, you can accept it for him. I've spelled out clearly that you are to take the first offer that works. Under the circumstances, I don't want you to delay acceptance, trying to improve terms."

Regan watched her closely. While Roya's distress seemed sincere, even in the midst of her angst, Regan noted, she had the wherewithal to tilt her head down slightly so she could gaze up guilelessly at Tom through long lashes as she managed a wan smile, and held out the envelope to him.

"Do you think that's wise?" Tom asked solicitously. "If you locate him, he may not appreciate being found. And now that you know he's disregarded how his actions might affect you, the fact that you've been close in the past might not protect you from him, especially if he feels cornered. It appears that he's killed two people already; he could be dangerous."

Roya threw back her scotch and rose, shoulders back and head held high until her posture fell into statuesque perfection.

"In many ways, he's my soul mate. It's a chance I'm willing to take," she said before she turned and left Tom's office.

Tom picked up his phone as soon as she was out of earshot and punched in a number. "I don't think she understands how much danger she could be in."

"Dave, it's Tom. Roya Matthews just left here. She said she's going to try and track down Mathius Hugel — she thinks he's fled to Mexico and she has an idea where he may have gone there — and I'm worried about her. Can you get a hold of the Capitola police and see if..." he went silent, listening to Dave's response.

"That's good to hear," he said finally, "very good to hear. Thanks, Dave."

"Dave says the Capitola police have already communicated with Mexican authorities. Roya told CPD she booked a flight from Monterey to Acapulco and gave them the flight number. They've already passed it along to the Acapulco police. They'll have someone ready to follow her when she gets off the plane in the hopes she'll lead them to Mathius Hugel, who can then be arrested and extradited back here to face murder charges. They won't be protecting Roya from Hugel, but the result will be the same."

"So, she's cooperating with the authorities to catch her 'almost soul mate'?" Regan asked quizzically.

"It sounds like she is."

Regan felt a disheartening flash of skepticism.

The police officer who appeared in their office the next day wasn't Dave. He introduced himself as Sargent Coby of the Capitola Police Department as he shook first Regan's hand and then Tom's.

"What can we do for you, Sargent Coby?" Tom asked.

"I understand you have a working relationship with one Roya Matthews?"

"That's right," Tom responded with a touch of concern in his voice. "Is she alright?"

"That's a good question, sir. We arranged for a local police officer to tail her when she disembarked in Acapulco, but she went into a lady's room at the airport and, according to him, never came out. The authorities there discovered her name on a flight manifest from Acapulco to Guadalajara that took off about forty-five minutes after her arrival, but by the time they discovered she had taken another flight, the plane had landed and all the passengers had dispersed."

"They lost her," Regan stated rather than asked.

"Yes, ma'am. It would appear she gave the Mexican authorities the slip."

Regan could feel heat in her cheeks. Of course Roya had. She never intended to cooperate with the authorities. Roya wasn't going to turn over her "soul mate." She was going to warn him, perhaps help him evade arrest. Roya's sob story about him ending himself was no doubt made up, too.

"We've checked with Ms. Matthews office in Carmel, but they don't have any more information about how to reach her than we do. We were sort of hoping against hope that you might have a cell number for her that we don't have or that she left information with you about how to contact her since you are doing some business with her."

"I'm sorry, Sargent," Tom apologized. "She turned over her listings to us so we are free to handle all that needs to be done without consulting her. Our only required future contact will be to send her a check when the listings she gave us close escrow."

Sargent Coby shook his head. "Brick walls everywhere. We think she probably planned to shake us from the start."

There was no probably as far as Regan was concerned; she was sure that was Roya's plan. "What happens now?"

"Her photo and description have been forwarded to the Guadalajara authorities, but it's a big city and she's not wanted for anything. Finding her is a low priority for them. It would take a lot of luck for her to be spotted; I'm not optimistic that we'll see her again until she wants us to. I just thought I'd check in with you to close every loop possible.

"Thanks for your time," Sargent Coby said politely. He shook hands with Regan and Tom again as he left.

16

Wednesday rolled around, and since offers had come in and quickly been been accepted on both Martha's and Judi's condos and Mireya's house — such was the market at the moment — both Tom and Regan were ready for a well-deserved day off from real estate responsibilities.

"I thought I'd be swamped and didn't set up a golf game for today," Tom complained. "Do you want to drive up the coast to Pescadero and hit Duarte's for some artichoke soup? We could grab a berry pie while we're there, too."

"If you swear spending time with me isn't just your backup plan and make it blackberry pie, I'll consider your proposal," Regan teased. "And could we make it two pies? I need one for Dave."

"Sure. The pie for Dave: is it a thank you pie or a future bribery pie?" Tom quizzed.

"Give me some computer time and then hopefully some time to make a few phone calls and I'll let you know."

"Now I feel like I'm your backup plan. What are you up to now, Sweetheart."

"It's a longshot, but I have an idea. If I can track down where Mathius Hugel and Roya grew up, I might find their parents or an old friend of one or both of them who knows where they like to go in Guadalajara. If I find anything out…"

"Longshot, alright, but I like it because playing on the computer and long-distance interviews can't get you in any trouble.

"I can't believe it's Wednesday, the sun is shining, and I don't have a round scheduled," Tom wailed, remembering his plight dramatically." How could I have let this happen?" He picked up his golf bag and patted it lovingly, adding a protracted sigh for effect. "I'm going through little white ball withdrawal, and if you insist on working instead of entertaining me, I think I'll at least hit the driving range and menace a bucket of my more loyal playmates. I'll leave you to your research and be back in time our road trip," he said as he gave her a kiss goodbye.

Regan had put in some effort trying to find out about Mathius Hugel's present day activities before without much success; he seemed to disappear a few years ago. But she had a new plan of attack. She wasn't going to search for Mathius Hugel in the present, she was going to look for Roya Matthew's in the past. Now that she knew Roya and Hugel had grown up together, she'd direct her search at Roya and hopefully follow her back to her girlhood, using her history as a way of finding about Mathius Hugel's childhood.

Regan entered "Roya Matthews" on her laptop. There were pages dedicated to successful Carmel realtor, Roya Matthews. She changed the parameters to "Roya Matthews

Connecticut," reasoning since Mathius Hugel's past put him in that state as a successful architect, that might be where he and Roya were from originally. Nothing came up. "*Humph*." Regan said to herself impatiently.

"*Ahh*," she quickly came up with another idea and attacked her problem from a different direction. Even though Roya said she hadn't been adopted by Mathius' family, she tried Roya Hugel. She found four references. All were women younger than the Roya she wanted and none of them were from Connecticut.

Regan drummed her ring finger on her desk, with the rest of her fingers hovering over her mouse. Finally, she decided to return to searching for "Mathius Hugel Connecticut architect," but to find his more distant past this time, rather than searching for him in the last few years. She was greeted by pages of listings. She decided to delete "architect." There were many pages with his name that came up even without the designation.

Regan carried her laptop to the kitchen and put water in the tea kettle. She had pulled up two of the pages and read them by the time the water boiled. She made her tea and resigned herself to reading all of the pages in the hope of finding what she needed, a task she wasn't looking forward to at all.

By the time Tom came home, she had finished three cups of tea, pulled her hair into a ponytail and wound it into a bun to keep hair from falling into her face as she bent over her laptop, bookmarked three pages that were somewhat interesting, and still didn't have anything of real consequence to show for her morning's efforts.

"You ready to go? Any luck?" Tom asked.

"Yes to your first question. No to your second one. Let me check one more entry and then, please, drag me away from the screen while I can still see."

Mr. Royce Hugel, 58, Regan read, *his wife Patricia, 57, and their son Mathius, 14, residents of Cornwall, were taken to Sharon Hospital by ambulance with non-life-threatening injuries following an accident on the Sharon Goshen Turnpike. According to police reports, the car the Hugel family was in was forced off the road by a vehicle driven by Mr. Darren Pike, 37, and overturned. Mr. Pike was cited for driving while intoxicated.*

The article was from the Cornwall Chronicle and dated November 15, 1982.

Regan cried out, "Tom, you're a magic man. I've been searching for a lead all morning without success. You walk through the door and the next thing I see is exactly what I was searching for."

"I'm an amazing guy alright," Tom laughed. "What exactly did I magically make appear?"

"Nothing less than the name of Mathius Hugel's adoptive parents, the town he grew up in, and his age. With that information, I should be able to track down people who knew him and Roya, too, when they were growing up. With any luck, I'll find their parents or at least someone who's kept in touch with one of them. Would you please come here and lay your magical hands on my laptop to make it so?"

"Ummum," he shook his head. "I'd be happy to lay my hands on you any time you want, but" he held his hands aloft and wiggled his fingers, "other than you, they touch nothing until it's a spoon at Duarte's. Let's go; I'm starving."

Regan and Tom drove up the coast some forty miles, enjoyed lunch, and had a leisurely walk around the delightful community of Pescadero, finishing their tour at the Pescadero Flowery to pick a bouquet of seasonal flowers and meet George, the cat.

"You'll be glad to hear that I'm hardly thinking about Roya and Mathius at all," Regan boasted to her husband as she bent to stroke the cat.

"Just enough that you have to remind yourself of that," Tom laughed. "I can tell it's time to get you back home."

Without Duarte's and charming boutiques to distract her, Regan's mind slipped back into investigative mode. If she could have paced in a car she would have. Instead, she fidgeted noticeably.

"I'm driving as fast as is safe, you know," Tom said.

"I know. It's just that going home seems to be taking so much longer than getting to Pescadero did."

Regan was back at her computer within two minutes of them getting home a little after 5:00. Her first discoveries were obituaries for both Royce and Patricia Hugel. They had reached their nineties and died within a week of one another — something she found terribly romantic — but their deaths meant she wouldn't have an obvious and easy starting point to trace Roya and Mathius.

The family had been small, with Mathius the only surviving relative listed amid a scattering of predeceaseds like parents and Royce Hugel's sister. Regan wondered as she read if the oversight of her name among the list of family members had troubled Roya or if she was already off in some other state and had not concerned herself with the official rules of who was considered formal family in small local newspaper obituaries.

Regan turned to school news stories next and found an article about Mathius's graduating class of eighth graders. *Thank goodness for small-town newspapers with a need to fill pages*, she smiled to herself. Since she didn't know if Roya was younger or older than her almost brother, Regan didn't bother trying to find a similar announcement for her. Instead, she tracked down two male names who were in Mathius's class who still lived in the Cornwall area and found phone numbers for them easily.

Next, she turned to property ownership records in Cornwall, Connecticut. The Hugel family had owned a house on the picturesquely alliterated street named Weeping Willow Way. By checking neighbors' records during the time of their residency and comparing them to current owners, Regan found a neighbor family who would have known the Hugels. She excitedly looked up their phone number.

Regan was about to call the neighbor's number when she realized it was a few minutes before 7:00 and that, with the time difference between California and Connecticut, she might wake up someone who was already asleep back East, especially since the neighboring family members would likely be seniors by now. Though she was excited about her discoveries and impatient to pursue her leads, she had no choice but to wait until the next morning to make her calls.

She started at 6:00 a.m. It would be a respectfully late-enough hour in Connecticut that she wasn't worried about making a too-early intrusion on her targets' day. She started with the most promising lead, the neighbors, but when she dialed their number, rather than a greeting, she got a busy signal.

She tried the next lead, one of Mathius's eight-grade classmates. An annoying sing-song of mechanical noises and a pre-recorded message informed her that the number she was calling had been disconnected. She had the same result with the second classmate's number. The research she had done must have turned up older landline numbers that had been abandoned in favor of unlisted cell phone numbers. There were times she hated cell phones.

Regan redialed the neighbors' number every half hour until she had to get ready for the Broker's House Tour that happened every Thursday, but was greeted by a busy signal each time she called. She consoled herself with the fact that a busy signal meant the number was active and that she'd reach her target eventually.

She got lucky as she sat outside the last house she wanted to preview on the morning tour.

"Yes," the voice that greeted her was female. It sounded older and slightly cautious.

"Mrs. Hamilton?"

"Who wants to know?

"My name is Regan McHenry…"

"You know I'm on a 'do not call list.' What are you selling this morning?

"I'm not selling anything, Mrs. Hamilton. I'm hoping you can answer some questions for me about some neighbors you had several years ago. The Hugel family?"

There was a silence that lasted long enough for Regan to prompt, "Do you remember them, Mrs. Hamilton?"

"Of course I remember them. What? Do you think I'm senile or something? What I'm trying to figure out is who you are and why you want to know about them. That, and if I should be talking to you at all since you didn't say you were following up on a call a last week from the Capitola Police Department in California. What business of yours is the Hugel family?"

So, the Capitola Police Department had used her reasoning and found a Hugel's family neighbor and interviewed them already. Knowing that, Regan felt much less clever than she had until that moment.

"If the Capitola Police Department contacted you, I'm sure they told you that Mathius Hugel is a murder suspect. I'm a friend of the woman, well, both of the women, he's accused of murdering."

"Ahh! Oh, my!" Mrs. Hamilton gasped audibly. "They didn't say that. No, they didn't say anything like that. They said they wished to speak to him as a person of interest — that's the term they used — in a local crime. I've watched enough TV crime shows to know that means suspect or maybe not, so I assumed maybe not. I'll be happy to answer your questions, but you must tell me all about what's happened."

With the promise of titillating detail, the woman was no longer worried about Regan's credentials. No doubt Mrs.

Hamilton's phone line had been busy for so long that morning because she was a gossip who enjoyed discussing, probably at some length, whatever might prove to be juicy. That made her just the person Regan hoped to reach.

"Shall I begin at the beginning?" Regan asked.

"Please do, and don't leave anything out for the sake of brevity."

Regan checked her watch and realized she was going to miss the last house on tour. She'd have to see it another time. She began at the beginning and left nothing out.

Mrs. Hamilton was an appreciative audience. Except for an occasional, "Oh, no." or "Oh, how shocking," she listened attentively as Regan filled her in on everything from Mathius's finding his mother and half-sister to male DNA under Judi's fingernails that likely belonged to him.

"Now it appears that he's escaped the country," Regan said. "He's a regular visitor to Mexico and I was hoping you might have kept in touch with him or know someone who has who might know where he's gone there."

"Me? Oh, no, I can't help you. It's been so long since his parents passed, and they were always a private family, never a family to invite neighbors over for drinks or weekend bar-b-ques. And after his parents died, well even before that, he didn't have anything to do with me or my late husband, especially not after he became a big-deal architect."

"What about friends? Do you remember any children he played with regularly? Perhaps your children or another neighbor's children have kept in touch?"

"Um, no. My children were much older than him so they didn't play with him. As I remember, he didn't have many friends; he wasn't a popular little boy. Now-a-days, you'd say he was bullied. Back then we would have said he was teased. Most of the neighborhood children thought he was strange and weren't friendly towards him. I must admit, I thought he was strange, too."

"Strange in what way?" Regan asked, certain that Mrs. Hamilton was about to manufacture some precursory peculiar behavior now that she knew that Mathius was likely a murderer.

"It's hard to say, exactly. He seemed very flamboyant. He liked to wear bright colored kind of flowy things, not the jeans and tee-shirts boys of his age wore. And he wore a scarf and a hat; he was never without his scarf and hat. Even in the heat of summer, he always wore a scarf of some sort and his hat wasn't an Indiana Jonesy sort of thing, either. The hat he wore had a big feather on it; like I said, flamboyant. No wonder he was teased. Of course, after he became a well-regarded architect, most people thought he liked to dress like that because he was artistic. Although," Mrs. Hamilton paused, "although he, well, he never seemed comfortable in his own skin. I always thought he was probably gay and that's what his outfits were really about."

"And what about Roya? Did she have any friends she might still be in touch with? She said both she and Mathius liked Mexico and had gone there together many times. She's gone after him. Perhaps one of her friends would know where they went when they traveled?"

"Roya?"

"Yes, Roya. The Hugel's other child."

"The Hugel's only had Mathius."

"I know they never officially adopted her, but she lived with them…"

"No." Mrs. Hamilton was adamant. "The Hugel's didn't have anyone else who lived with them. They just had Mathius."

"But Roya said Mathius and she were raised together…"

"I'm not senile or forgetful," Mrs. Hamilton stressed. "The Hugel's didn't have a girl who lived with them. Not ever."

Regan was so startled by what Mrs. Hamilton said that she was barely able to thank her for her time before she said goodbye.

No, she didn't think Mrs. Hamilton was forgetful. But what about the story Roya's told them of growing up with Mathius, and them being related, and her knowing him so well that they were almost soul mates. *Just what sort of game was Roya playing at, anyway?* Regan wondered.

Regan skillfully used a cell phone, an app that let her open lockboxes, paperless signatures on transmitted documents, and texting to keep in touch with clients, but the truth was that she never felt truly comfortable with technology. If she'd been older, she could have labeled herself a luddite and railed against it. If she was younger, it would have been second nature to her, but at forty-five she was a creature of an in between world: capable, but still uneasy and not interested in it. Besides, she had Tom with his programmer background and great knowledge and interest in technology to figure things out for her if she got stuck.

Unfortunately, Tom wasn't with her when she forgot to add a star to the security numbers at the Depot Hill house with huge ocean views she was showing her newly wealthy young buyer. The alarm she triggered was silent, and Regan didn't know she'd done anything wrong until two police officers showed up to see if she was attempting to break into the house. The officers were friendly, but one kept her hand on the handle of her holstered weapon for a good minute while Regan explained that she wasn't a criminal, but simply an inept real estate agent.

The only thing worse than her embarrassment and her client's nervous laughter was that one of the responding Capitola Police officers recognized her.

"Aren't you the same real estate agent who found that body in the Balboa Park condo? You're friends with Officer Everett in Santa Cruz, aren't you? Wait till I tell him what you did. He's gonna' get a belly laugh out of this," the policeman smirked.

"Is it absolutely necessary that you tell him what I did?" Regan asked lightly, chortling ever so slightly as she spoke.

His response wasn't lighthearted. "Yes, ma'am it is. You were careless and caused two patrol cars to be dispatched to the scene. Officer Everett may be able to explain — in a friendly way — why you need to be more careful in the future."

"Yes, I'm sure he will," a chastened Regan said. "Thank you, officer."

Dave turned up at her office later in the day. He stood leaning against her door-jam with his arms folded across his chest and a dour look on his face.

"I could take you down to the station house for a talking to since you're a repeat offender, but I'm feeling generous because of that blackberry pie you gave me a coupla' weeks ago, so I'm gonna' save you some public shaming — not gonna' make you do a perp-walk through your office to my car — and remind you to read your instructions carefully the next time you have a super high-end alarmed house to show some hot-shot buyer. Am I clear?"

Regan considered a sarcastic comeback, but opted not to argue. "Yes, Officer Everett," she said humbly. "I promise I'll be good."

Dave emitted a loud guffaw. "That would be a first. So, I hear your client didn't like facing down a couple of cops. He have a guilty conscience or something? Did he really bolt?"

Regan nodded. "I don't know if he feels guilty for making so much money when his company was purchased, but I do think I lost him as a client."

"He would have been a big commission, wouldn't he? They're asking what, three mil for that house?"

It was Regan's turn to look dour.

"I got some other info to tell you that should get your mind off him. Your favorite golden girl real estate agent got picked up in Cancun."

"Roya was arrested?"

"No, not arrested, just picked up, as in back on the Mexican authorities' radar. Looks like she booked a flight back to Monterey in a couple of days...alone. No sign of Mathius Hugel."

"Why am I not surprised?" Regan's words were sardonic. "And why do I have the feeling that she did find him in Guadalajara and warned him to stay in Mexico."

"She'll be getting a visit from CPD asking her all about her travels south of the border, you know, where she went, who she saw. If she did meet up with him, they'll get her to spill."

"I'm not so sure they will. She's good at being misleading; she may even be good at downright lying."

"You've jumped to that conclusion based on what? Other than giving the Acapulco police the slip — and since she didn't know she was being watched, that may have not been deliberate — I hear she's been cooperative."

"I had an interesting phone conversation with an old neighbor of the Hugel family back in Connecticut where Mathius grew up."

Dave tilted his head and squinted, suspicion written on his face.

"What?" Regan asked.

"How did you know where Mathius Hugel grew up? Does the Capitola Chief need to give a good talking to to someone on CPD staff about sharing information with a pesky real estate agent who asks too many questions she has no right to ask?"

"No one told me anything. I figured it out on my own; it wasn't hard."

There was a touch of admiration in Dave's tone. "Every once in a while I think you're in the wrong job."

"The neighbor woman I called told me quite a different story about Roya and Mathius than Roya did." Regan ran her tongue over her lips as she formulated a plan. "Roya's coming back in a couple of days is perfect timing. Escrow is closing on two referrals she gave Kiley and Associates. I think I'll be a very considerate fellow agent and take her commission checks to her, together with a bottle of champagne.

"She can tell me all about her search for Mathius. The CPD people and I can compare notes to see how consistent she..."

"Whoa. Stop right there. You and CPD aren't going to compare anything. I thought you just said you'd be good?"

"Okay, Okay." Regan held up her hands in a gesture of surrender. "I'll stay out of official police business. I'll just ask Roya about what Mrs. Hamilton had to say. I'm anxious to know who's telling the right story about Mathius's and her past." Regan leaned back in her chair and smiled.

"Definitely in the wrong job," Dave said. "Detective or workin' undercover would suit you better than sellin' houses. The other definitely in this is it's definitely not your concern. Your little pal Mireya seems to be in the clear and so are her male friends. Your dodgy vet didn't kill anyone, even if he may have bilked the SPCA for some unperformed or unnecessary surgeries, and your least favorite character, well, at least from Tom's perspective, maybe Roya Matthews bent some ethical rules but she didn't break any of them."

"You're forgetting one thing. My friend Martha was murdered and so was her friend Judi. The authorities haven't caught their killer and I still believe Roya knows where he is. One more attempt, Dave, give me one last chance to question her and, if I can't get anywhere, then I promise, I'll let it go."

"You won't have to 'cause Tom and I will do an intervention."

When Dave was on his way, Regan called Roya's Carmel office and asked her assistant when she expected Roya to be back at work. Dave's information was accurate. Roya would make her glittery return in three days. Regan set to work immediately. Since she was nearing the end of her tether, she had to get this final meeting right.

As she had done before, she got out the files for Mireya's and Martha's properties and pulled Roya's business card off the front of Mireya's folder. She didn't know why she did so exactly — it wasn't like she could absorb unknown information from a business card through her fingers — but somehow, she hoped staring at Roya's perfect image would inspire her thought process.

She noted the impressive list of Roya's real estate designations that ran down the left side of the card like alphabetically organized badges of honor and made a mental note of the time for classes and money Roya would have spent earning each of them. ABR and ACR: Accredited Buyers Representative and Accredited Sellers Representative, $500 each. ACRE: Accredited Consultant in Real Estate, $500. CRE: Counselor of Real Estate, $900. GRI: Graduate Realtor Institute, $1900. NAAB. Regan stopped. That was a designation she didn't recognize and yet the acronym was familiar. What did it mean; where had she seen it?

The realization hit her suddenly. National Association of Accreditation Board: NAAB. It was an architectural designation, the same high level one Mathius Hugel held. So Roya was a highly accredited architect, just like Mathius was?

Regan jumped on her computer, fingers typing so eagerly she missed hitting the keys she wanted and had to back up repeatedly. She typed in "roya matthews NAAB" and willed her computer to search faster than it ran. Although page after page of Roya Matthews as a real estate agent came up, there were no corresponding pages listing her as an architect.

She noted something else. Roya's history in real estate began about seven years ago, first in Connecticut and then in Carmel. If she remembered correctly, Mathius Hugel stopped updating his architecture pages about seven years ago. How had she missed that before?

Her mouth fell open in astonishment. She inhaled in a gasp and leaned back in her chair. To her adroit and imaginative mind, that coincidence answered so many questions.

🏠🏠🏠🏠🏠🏠🏠🏠🏠🏠🏠🏠

By the time Regan drove toward Carmel for her meeting with Roya, she was feeling powerful. She had done her research. Let Roya dress in gold and give an Academy Award worthy performance, it didn't matter. She was ready. But, although she felt confident her conclusion was right, she had to convey absolute certainty to Roya. She hadn't told her suspicions to anyone, not to Dave, and not even to Tom. Roya had to be the first to hear them.

She couldn't wait to confront Roya. She drove too fast. She didn't rehearse what she was going to say. She didn't need to. She knew her words would flow naturally, stinging librettos that would strip away Roya's dazzle.

When she had turned off her car engine in Roya's real estate office parking lot, she grabbed her chilled champagne in a chokehold around the bottle's neck and strode into the office, taking long confident steps.

"I'm here to see Roya," she announced to the receptionist.

"Oh yes. She's expecting you, Mrs. McHenry. I'll let her know you're here."

"There's no need. I know the way to her office and," she held up the champagne and waggled the bottle, "we're old friends."

Roya was sitting at her desk studying paperwork when Regan opened her door. Roya was wearing reading glasses, sensible dark rimmed glasses, not fashionable ones. As she peered over the top of them and recognized Regan, she yanked them off her nose with lightning speed and dropped them on her desk.

Regan smiled broadly. The always perfectly-turned-out-and-in-complete-control Roya had a self-perceived weakness that she didn't want Regan to see. The fact that she had gave Regan a small, but real advantage.

"Oh, Roya, Tom's not with me," Regan chuckled. "You don't need to take off your glasses for me. What's a pair of mundane reading glasses between us girls?"

Roya's hand smoothed her ever present scarf, pale pink today to match her elegant suit. "I am vain, aren't I?" Roya asked charmingly.

If Regan hadn't been so sure of what she thought Roya's truth was, she might have been beguiled by the self-deprecation in Roya's remark.

Regan replied with the faintest of smiles, letting her expression render judgment. "I brought your commission checks for Mireya's and Martha's property and some champagne for us to celebrate." She frowned deliberately. "How are you going to handle the cash from the sales now that Mathius has gone missing?" she asked innocently. "He is still missing, isn't he? You didn't find him in Mexico, did you?"

Roya shook her head. "I looked everywhere I could think of in Cancun and Acapulco, but there was no sign of him."

"What about in Guadalajara?" Regan kept her voice level and guileless. "You did go there looking for him, too, didn't you? In fact, you spent some time in that city, so you must have searched for him extensively…" Regan paused for several seconds, "or were you doing other things in Guadalajara? Maybe having a little surgery done?"

The sudden redness in Roya's cheeks made her already softly colored suit look a full shade paler. "I did look for him there for a while, but I'm embarrassed to admit it, you're right. I was having a tummy tuck and some body sculpting done."

"Oh. Is that what they call it?" Regan asked with surprise. "You didn't find him, though?"

"He found me," Roya dropped her eyes as she spoke, "at least he knew where I was because he sent me another message. It was…I guess you'd call it a suicide note. It was handwritten and said, by the time I read it, he would be dead. He confessed to killing Martha and her friend in it, too."

"Did he say why he killed them; did it give his motive?"

"No. It only said that he had to confess before he died."

"I imagine you'd keep such a note. Have you given it to the police?"

"I have. They met me at the Monterey airport and hustled me into custody for questioning. I'm exhausted. They questioned me non-stop for several hours until they were finally satisfied I was telling the truth. I guess that means they now accept that Mathius was a murderer and realize he will never be brought to justice. It's all so sad on so many levels."

"I assume the Capitola police will have their handwriting expert look at the note."

Roya met Regan's gaze again. "Handwriting expert?"

"Yes. I'm sure they'll have to authenticate his note. I bet they'll be asking you for any correspondence you had with Mathius for comparison."

Roya shrugged and shook her shoulders. "But I don't have anything long that he hand-wrote. We mostly communicated electronically. I only have his signature on various documents and some brief notes — words — he wrote on his blueprints for Martha Varner's house."

"Oh, she won't need a letter or anything like that. The handwriting expert the Capitola Police Department uses is a she, by the way. I know because I sold her a condo. She'll look at his signature on your contracts and at the blueprints he prepared. That should be all she needs. Of course, you know all about handwritten comments on blueprints since you're an architect yourself. You're such an accomplished woman," Regan said, attempting to sound genuinely awestruck, or at least impressed.

Roya didn't respond.

"I saw the NAAB designation on your business card with all your other designations," Regan added. *Your vanity again*, she thought.

"You know it's so fascinating about handwriting." Regan chattered on enthusiastically. "I saw something on PBS that explained even when someone goes to great effort to disguise their handwriting, a moderately talented analyst can find telltale strokes that give away the true writer's identity. Even if a right-handed person uses their left hand, for example, they can't completely disguise their writing. Isn't that interesting?"

"It is. So when they compare Mathius's writing on the note with the documents I have and his blueprint notes, they'll verify he wrote the note." Roya sounded relieved.

"They will," Regan said unequivocally. Then she sighed and looked perplexed. "I wonder if the Capitola Police Department analyst will look only at specific lines on documents or if her skilled eyes will take in other signatures in close proximity."

"What do you mean?"

Regan thought she detected the slightest discomfort in Roya's voice, but decided she might just be guilty of wishful thinking. She clarified, with a hard prod.

"Well, your signature will be right under Mathius's on some contracts, won't it? I wonder if a handwriting analyst would compare your signature to Mathius's without even meaning to," Regan raised her eyebrows, "or if it would take someone like me, for instance, mentioning it to her that she should?"

Other than a quick fluttering of her eyelashes, Roya's demeanor didn't change, but that reaction was enough to encourage Regan.

"I've spoken with an old neighbor of yours, Mrs. Hamilton. You remember her, don't you? She certainly remembered the Hugels and especially Mathius with his ever-present scarf, but the funny thing is, she didn't remember you. Her remembrances got me thinking. I looked up Mathius on my computer and compared when he stopped posting about his architectural work and then I looked you up, too, to see when your real estate career started. Funny, you and Mathius are kind of like Superman and Clark Kent, never seen at the same time.

"Now, you remember that you told Tom and me that Mathius borrowed your Blenheim Chevalier King Charles Spaniel for the Monterey Wag 'n Walk where he met Martha, but when I asked SPCA volunteers, none of them could remember seeing a man with a dog like that. Oh, they knew you had such a dog. They just couldn't remember a man with a dog like yours.

"Then when I heard you'd spent some time in Guadalajara, this weird thought crept into my mind, so I did some research. I bet you know all about GRS Mexico, where they do gender reassignments. Coming back so soon is pushing the recovery time they suggested for male to female surgery, but it's doable if there aren't any complications. Kudos to you, Roya. You must be a fast healer and a tough woman."

Roya was on her feet before Regan finished speaking, shaking with fury. "You're not implying…"

"You bet I am. You're a regular traveler to Mexico, probably not only to keep up your tan but for hormone injections. You killed Martha and Judi — there was a witness who saw you leaving Judi's condo — but since the DNA found under Judi's fingernails was male, everyone assumed it was Mathius impersonating you who killed her.

"And then there was your magnificent performance of being devastated that Mathius would try to implicate you in murder. Everyone bought it."

When Regan spoke again, there was compassion in her voice. "Something as physically difficult and permanently life changing couldn't have been a decision you made without a great deal of thought. How long had you been planning your surgery? How long had you been planning to let Mathius take the blame for murder? Most importantly, why? I assume you killed Judi because she might figure out who you were and what you did, but why did you kill your mother? Judi said Martha was so happy to have you back in her life. And you said Mathius had searched so hard to find her."

Roya sat down again and Regan assumed she had done so to be in a less taxing position physically as she confessed. Instead though, while Roya didn't deny what Regan charged, she took a completely different tack.

"Are you that jealous of me, Regan?" she asked coolly. "I know it drives you crazy that your husband finds me so attractive. I was having fun flirting with him, but after what you've just said, I'm going to take great pleasure in ruining your dull little life. Have you told him your incredible theory?"

"I thought you should be the first to hear what I know."

Roya sneered and made a sound that was close to a snarl. "Tell him whatever you like. It won't matter what you say to him. You can try to fight me for him, but you won't win."

Her eyes narrowed, but her voice was soft and calm. The lack of anger in her tone made her words even more menacing. "I'm going to take great pleasure in taking him from you right in front of your own eyes. Now get out of my office."

Regan rose silently and did as she was told. When she was in her car, she sat, hands on the steering wheel, and considered what had just happened. To her, Roya's lack of denial seemed like a confession. Roya had threatened to ruin her life by stealing Tom.

Most importantly, though, Roya was aware that Regan hadn't yet told anyone what she suspected. She'd read too many mysteries where the witness is killed immediately after making the phone call to the policeman on the case saying, "I have something important to tell you." She decided to correct that situation immediately.

She hit Dave's speed dial on her phone and was rewarded with a live response.

"Sup, Regan?"

"Will you be in your office in about an hour?"

"Plannin' to be."

"Then we have a date. I'm in Carmel, but I should be back by then. I'm coming straight to your office; no snacks or food bribes. I've just solved the murders of Martha Varner and her friend Judi, so I figure you owe me rather than the other way around."

"Whew!" Dave inhaled through pursed lips. "Then I better have some decent coffee ready for you."

"Seriously, Dave. I have all the puzzle pieces put together. And they all fit without the use of force."

"Peet's," Dave said as he reached across his desk and handed Regan a tall coffee encased in styrofoam. "With too much cream and sugar in it, just the way you like it. Sit and talk to me." He motioned her to the chair facing him on the other side of his desk.

Regan didn't need any encouragement. "You remember I told you about my conversation with Mrs. Hamilton, the Hugel's neighbor?"

"Yeah," Dave said tentatively. It took him a few seconds to recall who Mrs. Hamilton was and what conversation Regan alluded to, but once he did, his hesitation went away.

"And you remember that she said she didn't remember every seeing Roya Matthews in the household, even though Roya said she and Mathius grew up together?"

Dave nodded.

"Well, I was looking up background information about Roya and discovered she's an architect, not only an architect but a NAAB architect just like Mathius is."

"What's special about being an NAAB architect?"

"It's a prestigious and select group. Just being an architect doesn't get you in."

"OK."

"So I remembered I couldn't find any current information online about Mathius after about seven years ago. Curiously, when I started looking up Roya, I found tons of information about her..."

"I feel a 'but' coming here."

"But I couldn't find any information about her before about seven years ago.

"Mathius may have been seen briefly by some people in Carmel early on, but it would have been easy enough for Roya to impersonate him just like the Capitola Police think he impersonated her the day Judi was murdered."

"So, you're sayin' Mathius and Roya are the same person?" A smile spread across Dave's face until he hardly had any cheeks left. "You think when Roya Matthews wants to kill someone, she Mr. Hydes Mathius Hugel and when Mathius wants to go into hiding, he Dr. Jekylls Roya Matthews?"

"It's more complicated than that. They are the same person, or they were, but Mathius was transsexual and now he's become who he thought he was supposed to be all along, which is Roya.

"Roya has a history of going to Mexico..."

"With Mathius."

"She may have gone there under either identity, but I believe she was receiving hormone therapy there and getting ready to make a full transition. I also think she picked up insulin in Mexico. It's easy to do. You can get it over-the-counter and don't even need a doctor's prescription if you know where to go. That's how she procured her murder weapon.

"Roya said she was going to look for Mathius in Cancun and Acapulco, the cities she usually went to when she was in Mexico…"

"With Mathius."

"…or as Mathius. But as soon as she landed, she took a flight to Guadalajara, ostensibly to search for Mathius. Do you know what's in Guadalajara?"

"You're going to tell me, aren't you?"

"A world-renowned gender reassignment center. I read what's involved in transitioning from male to female. It's pretty rough..."

Dave involuntarily dropped his hands to cover his groin.

"…but if nothing goes wrong post-op, newly reassigned women can expect a recovery to the point of returning home within about two weeks, which is the length of time Roya spent in Guadalajara, not searching for Mathius, but in a hospital setting recovering from surgery."

"I hear Mathius wrote a confession that Roya gave to CPD."

"Yes. Roya said he wrote a note to her before he died. In her mind, that may have been exactly right because Mathius is no more. In a way, he died in Mexico, finally and completely. Now there's truly only Roya left."

"I don't know, Regan," Dave's words were skeptical, but his body slumped at his desk as if defeated and his demeanor said something else.

"There are two parts of Mathius that nothing will erase: his handwriting and his male DNA. Can't CPD start by having the writing in the note compared with something Roya's written? Oh, and I may have made up a little story that I told Roya about them having an on-staff handwriting expert that I know because I sold her a condo," Regan giggled, "but couldn't they find someone to do that?"

"Your story about being a real estate whiz may be off, but the county authorities do have a handwriting expert that we use regularly, so you weren't completely off base. So, yeah, the handwriting part can be done, but unless Roya is charged, we can't compel her to donate a DNA sample."

"But if the handwriting analysis proved she wrote the Mathius note, wouldn't a judge consider issuing some sort of warrant or demand? Couldn't someone with a lot more skill and resources than I have track Roya's movements in Mexico sufficiently to prove where she was and what I think she was doing there? She's probably undergone some lead-up surgeries too. I bet this wasn't her first trip to Guadalajara."

Dave's shrug was noncommittal.

"Talk to your connections at CPD — maybe start with that officer who chastised me for setting off the alarm — and don't let Roya Matthews get away with murder.

"Thanks for the coffee, Dave," Regan said as she put her untouched beverage on his desk.

She continued on to her office, relieved that someone she trusted and respected now knew what she was convinced was true. Dave might hesitate for few minutes, but she knew he was a man dedicated to justice and that if he did, it would only be to work out how to best present what she told him to the right people. The murders of Martha and Judi would be solved.

Roya's comment about stealing Tom hadn't given her pause. She was certain about the state of their marriage, even if she was the tiniest bit jealous of Roya's seeming perfection and Tom's appreciation of it. As she drove, though, she began looking forward to how she was going to tell him Roya may have been a woman at heart, but that she began life as a baby boy.

🏠🏠🏠🏠🏠🏠🏠🏠🏠🏠🏠

"How sure are you about your 'Mathius is Roya' and vice versa thing?" Dave asked unceremoniously when she answered her phone.

"Pretty darn sure. Why?"

"My buddy at CPD told me one of their officers asked Ms. Mathews if she would be willing to part with a few cells from inside her cheek and she said, 'Sure.' He offered her the option of going in to see one of Carmel's finest for the swab, but she declined, said she liked Capitola and had some unfinished business to take care of up here. She's comin' up tomorrow afternoon to do the deed. See, now to me, that doesn't sound like she's worried she's gonna' test he."

Regan was better at sounding confident than she was at feeling confident. After Dave hung up, she went over the confrontation she'd had with Roya in her Carmel office. Roya was furious and promised to take Tom away from her, but she never denied what Regan accused. To Regan, that lack of denial was as good as a confession, but as she replayed their skirmish, Regan began to wonder.

Was Roya answering with chillingly controlled rage and threats because of resentment, rather than because of fear or guilt? Was it possible Roya was angry solely because Regan had made such a wild assertion? Did she really have any proof behind her allegation or had she pieced together a bunch of circumstantial, or worse yet coincidental, oddities and decided they were evidence?

She'd been there before when she had to consider how to apologize after she'd been so sure Roya had defrauded Martha Varner, but if she was wrong this time, there were no words, no form of apology that could make up for accusing Roya of murder, especially when she had made Roya a changed version of Mathius.

"You're quiet tonight, Sweetheart," Tom said as their dinners were brought to their table at Mosaic.

"It's hard to talk over the belly dancer's music." Regan smiled at her husband, glad he was paying more attention to her than to the young dancer wriggling her way around the diners' tables.

He flashed a quizzical look her way, not about to let her get away with blaming the dancer for her silence.

"You're right. I'm second guessing and wondering what I'll say to Roya if I'm mistaken about her."

"I'm betting you're not wrong. In fact, I'm so sure that I'll take care of any apologies, if they're needed."

"What will you say to her?"

217

"I'll be humble and say how devastated you are about your mistake, and then I'll throw myself at her and let her have her way with me to make it up to her," he winked.

Regan was forced to smile. "Sometimes you are a wicked tease," she laughed.

"Why do you think I'm teasing?"

The belly dancer neared their table and leaned backwards in front of Tom, her hands held high above her head, undulating in the air. When she straightened up, she moved closer to him and began flipping a hip in his direction, sending the coins on her low-slung belt dancing more wildly than she was.

"Stuff a bill in her costume at your own peril." Regan took a turn at teasing.

The dancer moved on hoping the next table where three young men were ogling her and waving bills in the air would prove more lucrative.

As the belly dancer moved past their table Tom said, "I feel guilty not tipping her. She's probably working on a degree at UCSC or maybe going to Five Branches University, studying acupuncture."

"I'm sure she is," Regan laughed heartily, but her newly merry mood didn't last. "At least we'll know about Roya soon" she said, somber once again.

🏠🏠🏠🏠🏠🏠🏠🏠🏠🏠🏠🏠

Checking the clock when she knew Roya was scheduled to be interviewed at CPD was becoming routine for Regan. She began doing it every few minutes once 12:00 had passed and the morning officially became afternoon. Dave hadn't said when Roya was due to take her DNA test, only that it was going to be later in the day. She expected him to call any minute saying Roya had cancelled, but her phone remained silent. When the clock reached 4:50, she called him.

"Dave Ever…"

"Did Roya show up?" she asked before he was able to complete saying his name.

"I assume so. At least no one called to say she didn't. And I asked my pal at CPD to let me know if there was a hiccup in her plans because I knew you'd be all over me wanting to know."

"How long for the results to come in?"

"Depends on what's in line at the lab in front of your buddy Roya's test. Shouldn't be more than a day or two, though."

"You'll let me know if you hear anything?"

"I'd never hear the end of it if I didn't hit speed dial the second I know anything, would I?"

"No, you wouldn't."

Regan's phone beeped call waiting.

"I've got another call, Dave. Thanks."

"I'm about to take Tom from you just like I promised, but I knew you'd want to say goodbye so I'll give you a chance."

She knew the voice on the phone. Her heart raced. "Roya, what do you mean?"

"You know how much Tom loves his golf, don't you?" Roya giggled coquettishly. "I thought it would be fitting…but we can talk about that later. Not too much later, though.

Tom's sleeping now, but if he wakes up, I'll have to give him another injection. I'm very good with needles, but I've never needed to figure out how much is too much before, so you wouldn't want to be tardy and make me goof and overdose him."

"Roya…"

"Shut your mouth and listen," Roya's tone had changed from light and playful to cold and harsh. "Find Shakespeare Street on your GPS. Oh, it might not be on there. I don't know if it's a real street or if they just have the sign up because of Santa Cruz Shakespeare. Oh, well, you're such a clever woman, I'm sure you'll figure it out. I drive a gold Cadillac. When you spot it, park there and look toward the pond. One more thing: come alone or I won't give you a chance to say goodbye."

"Roya, Roya!" Regan screamed at her phone, but her taunter had ended the call.

Should she do as Roya said and come alone or should she take a chance and call Dave? She needed to make that decision quickly. Was it possible that Roya was bluffing or trying to set her up for a deadly meeting? Indecision immobilized her body as her mind frantically searched for the right answer.

Regan grabbed her purse and bolted from her office. She ran down the central hall to catch Amanda at the reception desk before she left at 5:00. As she passed Tom's open office door, she glanced in, hoping to see him sitting there. His office was empty.

"Amanda, Tom isn't here. I thought he was meeting with our agents for performance evaluations this afternoon. Do you know why he left? Did he say where he was going this afternoon?"

"Yes. He got a call from some hot buyer who wanted to see his listing on North Branciforte and had me postpone his meetings."

Regan grabbed the edge of the reception desk as a wave of panic washed across her. Roya wasn't bluffing and this wasn't a setup. She had Tom. "Amanda, you can't leave yet. I need your help."

"Sure, Regan. Are you okay? You look as white as a ghost."

"No. I'm not okay. I need paper and a pen."

Amanda produced what Regan requested and she scribbled a message on the sheet of paper, folded it in quarters, and handed it to Amanda.

"Please, you have to do exactly as I say. Don't read this now. Open it in fifteen minutes, call my friend Dave, and read it to him. I've put his office, cell, and home number on it. He'll be at one of those numbers."

Amanda looked frightened. "Regan, what's going on?"

"Don't ask. Just promise you'll follow my instructions exactly."

"Okay. Yes, I promise."

Regan turned and raced down the office hall to the back door and then out to the office parking area. She got in her car and tried not to shake. She had to be in control by the time she reached Roya.

Regan drove against Santa Cruz evening commuter traffic on Mission Street and hit the stoplight where Mission turned to the freeway on green. She stayed on Mission Street as it changed names and became Water Street when it passed downtown. She drove past the County Building and continued up the hill to Branciforte where she made a left turn. Her timing was about right. The drive so far had taken just under ten minutes.

She drove a little too fast on Branciforte as it left densely residential areas and became more rural. When she passed the house displaying a Kiley and Associates sign with Tom's name rider on it, she started to shake again.

Small arrowed signs pointed the way to the DeLaveaga Golf Course and she turned to follow them. She slowed as she reached the course, mindful of the cart crossings bisecting the road and fairways on either side of her. At twenty minutes after five the sun wasn't setting yet, but it had dropped behind tall trees that dotted the course and the fairways were losing light and deep in shadow. Even die-hard golfers wouldn't be starting their game in such fading light.

Regan drove past the clubhouse and Lodge Restaurant. There were a scattering of cars remaining in the parking lot, probably belonging to employees closing up and a straggler or two nearing the final hole and trying to finish their round before the light deserted them completely, but the pro shop had closed for the day and the Lodge, which was undergoing a renovation, was dark.

She drove on. On her right, she could see the beginnings of the pond. It was not a pristine body of water, not even a dark and foreboding body as it might have been as blue turned to black in the low light. Instead, its long expanse was covered in green algae, which glowed almost phosphorescent in the sun's fading rays, a dismal swamp, primordial and rank in the dwindling light. Water reeds grew upright out of it, decorating it in clumps, charming in daylight possibly, but in Regan's mind and the angled sunlight, forming hiding places for watery predators.

The sunlight was low enough that her headlights came on, one of the automatic features of her car, and as she drove on, a small blue sign with white letters reading Shakespeare was visible in their light. Regan slowed and put on her right turn blinker even though no one was on the road behind her to see it.

Twenty yards down the Shakespeare Road, she saw a gold Cadillac pulled off the pavement and parked in a wide expanse of natural terrain. It had to be Roya's car; Regan pulled in behind it. As she got out of her car, she heard the plop of a golf ball landing on a dip in the fairway below her, but whoever hit it was far enough away that, if the golfer made any comments about his lie, they didn't reach her ears.

Shakespeare Road had brought her back towards the clubhouse complex and what must have been the final green of the course, which was up a small grade beyond her. A low ridge enclosed the fairway and separated it from the end of the pond, which stretched from just past the clubhouse to Shakespeare Road. She scanned the area. "Tom," she shouted.

"We're down here by the pond," Roya called out to her, swinging the hand she held over her head back and forth in a dramatic wave. Regan could see Roya clearly. She glistened as the remaining sunlight hit the metallic threads of her head-to-foot golden outfit and caught her fluttering matching long scarf.

Roya motioned for her to come closer. "Careful where you walk," Roya yelled cheerily. "They've lopped off a bunch of saplings that were hiding the pond from view and the remaining ends are sharp, almost like daggers."

As she moved down the slope, a golf cart came into view. It was stopped on a steep incline a few feet above the edge of the pond, its front end aimed toward the murky water. Although it had a roof-like covering, it was open on all sides and a slumped figure was clearly visible inside it. "Tom!" Regan cried.

"That's right, Regan. Darling Tom is here. Oh, don't worry. He's only sleeping. I am sorry I had to hit him over the head when he came inside that house he thought he was going to sell me, but I gave him a little shot of something to help him rest, so he hasn't felt a headache or anything like that."

Roya dropped a hand to the very bottom of her stomach and rubbed. "He's a big man. I think I strained something, I may have even popped a stitch, getting him into my car. I was careful, too. I parked my car in the garage so I could load him in privately and take my time with him." She shook her head despairingly. "I do think that's when I did it, though, not when I transferred him to the golf cart I 'borrowed' from the return area.

"It's interesting. Golfers are so careless about leaving the keys in those things when they return them — don't you think I'm overdressed for golf?" she chuckled — "but no one seemed to notice me when I drove away with a cart and came here.

Regan had picked her way through the small stumps on the bank as Roya complained and had reached the back of the golf cart.

"That's close enough," Roya held up her left hand, signaling Regan to stop. In her right hand, Regan could make out a syringe. "If you come any closer, I'll jam this in his arm and put him to sleep forever."

"Roya, don't hurt him. Please," Regan begged.

"Oh, but I have to eventually. Still, I'm a woman of my word and I told you you'd have a chance to say goodbye to him as long as you came alone. You didn't tell anyone about our little rendezvous, did you?"

"I came alone, just like you asked."

"Good girl. For that maybe I'll let you give him a final kiss."

"I know you're doing this to get even with me. He didn't do anything to you. Take me instead." Regan pulled up her sleeve and held her arm out to Roya.

Roya laughed. "That would be much too easy for you. I want you to know what it's like to be alone like I was, to know it's your own fault, and to feel the pain that comes with that."

"I don't understand why you killed Martha. You weren't alone anymore. You found your mother and you even have a sister. You were in sight of being who you should have been. You had a family who loved you. Why did you give all that up?"

"You sound just like my mother," Roya spit out her words contemptuously. "She said we could all be one big happy family now: her, me, and my little sister. She even wanted us to live together in a triplex and asked me to design one for us. So why did I give that up? I gave it up because I hated them. My mother got rid of me because I wasn't the darling little girl she wanted. The irony, of course, is that I was; she just didn't wait until she could see that. She gave me away the moment she discovered I was born a boy. She needed to be punished for rejecting me."

"Roya, your mother didn't give you up because you weren't what she wanted. She was extremely young and alone when she had you. I'm sure she gave you up because she thought someone else could give you a better life than she could."

"Really? She kept my sister. How I hate Mireya, my mother's little miracle. She got all my mother's love. She got to live the childhood that should have been mine. I didn't want her to die for that, because it was my mother's fault not hers, but I wanted her to know what it feels like when your mother loves another child and not you, and she learned what that's like when she lost her house.

"It was fun for a while, setting her up to look like our mother's killer, too. I got to watch her being miserable and blamed for something that wasn't her fault, just like I was blamed for not being born a girl." Roya smiled at her memory.

"Now I am sorry about that other woman, but she knew too much. Eventually she might have figured things out," Roya's eyes narrowed, "just like you did.

"I planned every move out so carefully. I would have gotten away with all of it, too, if you had minded your own business. My mother would have paid for her sins and

Mathius would forever be blamed for her murder. And I could have been Roya for the rest of my life, as I always was intended to be."

Regan inched down the side of the golf cart toward Roya like she was playing a game of red-light-green-light as Roya vented.

"None of this had to happen to you and especially not to Tom. I feel particularly bad about him; I really liked him, you know. If you had just stopped poking around where you didn't need to be — if you hadn't told people that I had been Mathius — we could all have had bright futures. You and Tom could have been happy instead of ending up like this. Now it's too late for all of us."

"But you killed two people. How could I ignore that?"

"I didn't kill anyone. Mathius did."

"You're planning to kill Tom, Roya. You. Not Mathius; he's no more. Tom's death will be on you."

Regan's words hit a nerve. Roya wavered just a bit, still holding the syringe, but letting it drop to her side. It was the chance Regan hoped for and the only one she was going to get. She charged at Roya and grabbed her arm, twisting it hard until the syringe fell from her hand. Regan stomped on it and heard a satisfying crunch.

Roya screamed more in anger than in pain from what Regan had done to her and pushed her toward the back of the golf cart. Roya reached into the cart across Tom's slack body and turned it on. Then she released the cart's brake.

The cart hummed softly and began a decent toward the pond. As the cart moved past her, Regan bolted to its other side and grabbed Tom's arm, trying to pull him out of the cart before it reached the water. Roya took hold of Tom's other arm and held him fast in the moving vehicle as the front end reached the water. She leaned inside and braced herself with a knee on the seat, and began using both hands to drag the unconscious Tom toward her.

Regan screamed as the front wheels of the cart disappeared into the pond and dark green water began covering its nose. The pond seemed alive, like a beast slowly but inexorably devouring its prey. She pulled harder on Tom's arm but Roya's grip was unrelenting. She could feel him slipping away from her as he and the cart began to submerge in the muck. If she let him go, she would never find him in the algae darkened water.

Regan slid into the ooze and tried to dig in her heels, but the cart pulled her forward beyond where she tried to brace and hold herself. The mucky land gave way beneath her feet and she fell to her knees. Her hand slipped down Tom's arm toward his hand.

The water was up to Tom's waist. It floated his body ever so slightly, making his weight less. Lightened a bit, her grasp on his arm, tenuous as it was, began to move him toward her. She managed to get her right hand on his arm, too, and she pulled with more strength than she knew she had.

The cart was still descending, and as it did, it tipped away from her. Both she and Tom were fully in the water with only their heads above it, but Tom was free, no longer being held in the cart by Roya, and she managed to tug him out between the seat and roof of the cart. As she pulled, Regan peered under the cart roof and saw Roya, also outside the cart more or less in the same position they were in for a second before the water closed over the top of her head and she disappeared.

Regan's feet no longer found anything even marginally solid to touch. She kicked frantically while she tried to keep Tom's head above the slime. Her efforts cost her. She had just enough time to gulp a breath of air and close her eyes against the thick algae before her head was covered, too.

Tom rose away from her abruptly and his movement made her efforts at swimming productive. Her head broke the water line, she opened her eyes, and took an overdue deep breath.

"I've got him," Dave, chest high in the water, shouted to her. "I've got him."

More of Dave emerged and Tom floated toward shore, pulled by his chin which was cradled in Dave's sure hand. Regan followed awkwardly in bits, stumbling and falling into the slimy water more than once, but eventually reaching shore.

"You okay?" Dave asked.

"Yes. Is Tom…"

"He's breathing. Help me with him."

Together they dragged Tom fully out of the pond. "Backup's on the way, but he needs an ambulance. I'll call for one," Dave said as he began scrambling up the slope.

He had only gone a few feet when two men appeared at the top of the ridge. "Shall I call 911?" one of them asked, digging in his pocket for his cell phone.

"Absolutely," Dave replied "ask for an ambulance."

It was only after she knew Tom was still alive and that help was coming that Regan realized Roya wasn't on the bank with them. "Roya. Dave, where's Roya?"

"Making her great escape would be my guess."

"I saw her go under water."

"Wouldn't be the first time she's disappeared and turned up somewhere else, maybe even as somebody else."

Uniformed officers appeared from Shakespeare Road and charged down the slope. The light was far enough gone that they needed flashlights to see well and avoid the sapling stumps.

Dave called out to them. "We're good here. Get a perimeter around the pond. A woman looking like a swamp creature should be climbing out of it somewhere. She tried to kill these two."

The officers reversed course and relayed the message to other newly arriving police, who scattered at a quick clip, aiming their flashlights at the pond and swinging them in broad arches.

Tom moaned and his eyes fluttered, not quite opening.

"Tom, my love," Regan bent over him and kissed his cheek.

"Don't suffocate him," Dave commanded. "Don't scare him either. If he opens his eyes and sees his beautiful wife has turned into an alien swamp dweller, he's gonna' faint dead away."

Dominican Hospital wasn't far away and distant sirens from an ambulance dispatched from there grew distinct within a matter of minutes. Finally, Regan could see their flashing lights racing along the far side of the pond. The ambulance's earsplitting siren and red-flashing lights were things of beauty to her.

By the time the paramedics had carried Tom to the waiting ambulance, checked him over, and made sure he was stable, the golf course was dark and the pond appeared black and so calm, it reflected the night's stars and crescent moon like a mirror. The roof of the golf cart which had remained visible just above the waterline for a long time had finally slipped beneath the surface.

The lead officer listened intently as Dave filled him in with the rough details of what had happened. He made the decision to wait for morning light before trying to locate the golf cart, which he guessed was seeking the lowest point in the pond's center, before trying to hoist it out, agreeing that the highest and best use of his officers' time now was continuing to search for where Roya had emerged from the pond.

Regan overheard the charge officer reassuring Dave that they'd find her with a biting, "Where's she going to go, all green and slimy? She won't be able to hide and we've got her car. Even the golf carts are in their barn and locked up for the night. There's no way she can escape."

"You want to ride with him, ma'am?" One of the paramedics asked Regan, pulling her away from her eavesdropping.

"Definitely."

He pulled a Mylar blanket out of the ambulance gear box and wrapped it around her. "This is partly for you because you're starting to shiver," he grinned, "and partly because I don't want what's on you on the seats of my nice clean ambulance."

The paramedic offered her a hand and helped her up into the ambulance and then followed her inside. "He's out, but his vitals look good," he reassured Regan.

🏠🏠🏠🏠🏠🏠🏠🏠🏠🏠🏠

By the time Dave turned up in Tom's hospital room the next morning, Regan had been allowed to shower and given a pair of scrubs to wear by one of the sympathetic nurses, and her clothing had been consigned to the hospital dumpster.

Tom was sitting upright when Dave walked in, the effects of what Roya had given him had passed from his system.

"So," Dave greeted him, "how's it feel to owe your life to your wife?"

"Normal. I wouldn't have a life if she wasn't in it."

"Whacked on the head, given so much phenobarbital you almost didn't make it, and practically drowned, and you still know what to say to make anything the rest of us guys could come up with seem like we're cavemen."

"I'll do better once my head stops hurting."

"He has a mild concussion," Regan explained. "Did you find Roya?"

Dave could hear the anxiety in her voice. He rolled his tongue over his teeth and made a sucking sound before he spoke. "Yeah, about her…"

"You've got to catch her, Dave. I think she'll try again."

He shook his head slowly. "She's not gonna' come after Tom, or you, or anybody, again."

"Could you explain what you mean?" Tom asked, recovered sufficiently to be alert to the implication of Dave's statement.

"We didn't find her last night, but this morning, when we pulled the cart out of the pond, we did."

Regan frowned, "What?"

"You said you saw her go under the water," Dave answered and then shrugged. "You ever hear of Isadora Duncan?"

"The dancer who was killed when her scarf...oh my golly. Her scarf..."

"Must have gotten wrapped around the front wheel well when she was trying to keep Tom in the cart. You know those carts don't have good fenders and the wheels are near their edge. Both ends of her scarf got twisted up with the wheel and evidently she couldn't get it loose and she couldn't get it off her neck, either. She got pulled into the pond when the cart sank. They will be an autopsy so we'll know if she was strangled or drowned, but it doesn't matter much 'cause either way she's dead.

"All of a sudden Roya's DNA test is of great interest. It's been bumped to the front of the line. Results should be in later today. It's probably gonna' show she's a killer."

Regan spoke evenly and with certainty. "It will show she's the killer. Her DNA will be a match for the male DNA on Judi's body. There's no question at all in my mind about that."

"If that's the case, maybe justice was done, don't you think? I wouldn't feel sorry for her. And it's not like she had a great future in front of her. She'd probably spend the rest of her life in jail."

"I don't see someone like Roya, with her sparkling clothes and perfect makeup and hair, being happy in a jail jumpsuit," Tom added.

"Yeah. Goin' down with the ship — well, golf cart — may have been the best thing that could happen to her, under the circumstances."

Regan reached for Tom's hand and sighed loudly. "I know she killed two people — well, maybe in her mind it wasn't her at all, but Mathius who did that — and nothing that happened to her in her youth can justify what she did, but there was so much pain in her existence. And her end just adds to it. What makes it worse is her life had finally come together. If she hadn't…her life story could have had a happy ending."

"I look at it differently than you do, Sweetheart. Her life was always," Tom searched for the word he wanted, "unconventional. Her mother gave her up for adoption, but it sounds like she had loving adoptive parents. She had talent and skill and excelled in her profession, in both professions she chose, in fact. Most importantly, she may have struggled with her identity, but she was strong enough to know who she was and take action to make her body match her heart. Her problem was that even with all that, she chose the wrong wolf."

"The wrong wolf?" Dave looked puzzled.

"It's an old bit of Cherokee wisdom," Tom answered. "According to Cherokee lore, a grandfather explained to his grandson that there are two wolves struggling inside each of us. One wolf is vengefulness, anger, resentment, self-pity, and fear. The other wolf is compassion, faithfulness, hope, truth, and love. When his grandson asked, 'Grandfather, which wolf wins?' his grandfather replied, 'The one you feed'.

"In the end, Roya chose to feed the wrong wolf and it cost her everything."

"But growing up as Mathius…" Regan started to defend Roya.

"Interesting," Dave said. "I don't know about wolves, but the way I see it, she was always Roya and it was Roya who made those choices. What she chose hurt other people. I'm old school, but in my world, it's right to pay for your crimes."

Nancy Lynn Jarvis

About the author

Nancy Lynn Jarvis was a Santa Cruz, California, Realtor® for more than twenty years before she fell in love with writing and let her license lapse.

After earning a BA in behavioral science from San Jose State University, she worked in the advertising department of the San Jose Mercury News. A move to Santa Cruz meant a new job as a librarian and later a stint as the business manager for Shakespeare/Santa Cruz at UCSC.

Nancy's work history reflects her philosophy: people should try something radically different every few years, a philosophy she applies to her writing, as well. This is the seventh book in the Regan McHenry Real Estate Mysteries series but she has taken breaks to write a stand-alone book called "Mags and the AARP Gang" about a group of octogenarian bank robbers, and to edit "Cozy Food: 128 Cozy Mystery Writers Share Their Favorite Recipes."

She's also edited an anthology of short stories from Santa Cruz authors with the title and theme "Santa Cruz Weird."

For writers being noticed in the market place is always challenging, but you as a reader can help enormously by spreading the word.

So, if you have enjoyed this book as much as I enjoyed writing it, please help promote it and other Good Read Publishers and Good Read Mysteries titles.

There's a wide range of ways you can do so including:

- Recommending the book to your friends
- Posting a review on Amazon or other book websites
- Reviewing it on your blog
- Tweeting about it and giving a link to our website at www.nancylynnjarvis.com
- Suggesting the book to your book club
- Posting a comment on your Facebook page
- Pining a book on Pinterest
- Liking /ReganMcHenryRealEstateMysteries on Facebook
- Pinning books on Pinterest
- Anything else you can think of!

Many thanks for your help - it's much appreciated.

Good Read Publishers and Nancy Lynn Jarvis.

Follow Regan McHenry Real Estate Mysteries on Facebook at
www.facebook.com/ReganMcHenryRealEstate Mysteries
or
Visit Nancy Lynn Jarvis' website
www.nancylynnjarvis.com

Read the first chapter of the books by Nancy Lynn Jarvis, ask Nancy questions, and learn about what she's writing now.

Review reader comments and email your own.

Find out about upcoming events, book club discounts, and arrange for Nancy to talk to your book club or group.

Find out how to get copies of her books inscribed to give as gifts.

Books are also available for your Kindle, iPad, and other e-readers.